Pitkin County Library

120 North Mill Street
Aspen, Colorado 81611

DATE DUE

JAN 1 9 2005	
8/19/05	
AUG 24	
July 15	
3/24/12	

GAYLORD   PRINTED IN U.S.A.

The Thief Who Couldn't Sleep

LAWRENCE BLOCK

The Thief
Who Couldn't Sleep

A DIVISION OF

OTTO PENZLER BOOKS

NEW YORK

Introduction copyright © 1994 by Lawrence Block
Copyright © 1966 by Lawrence Block

Reprinted by permission of Knox Burger Associates Ltd.

Otto Penzler Books
129 W. 56th Street
New York, NY 10019
(Editorial Offices only)

Macmillan Publishing Company
866 Third Avenue
New York, NY 10022

Maxwell Macmillan Canada, Inc.
1200 Eglinton Avenue East, Suite 200
Don Mills, Ontario M3C 3N1

Macmillan Publishing Company is part of the Maxwell Communication Group of Companies.

Library of Congress Cataloging-in-Publication Data
Block, Lawrence.
     The thief who couldn't sleep / by Lawrence Block.
         p.   cm.
     "The Armchair detective library."
     ISBN 1-56287-064-5 (trade ed.)—ISBN 1-56287-063-7 (limited ed.)
     1. Tanner, Evan (Fictitious character)—Fiction.   2. Intelligence service—United States—Fiction.   I. Title.
     PS3552.L63T4   1994   93-40996   CIP
813'.54—dc20

Fiction
Block
Thi
604

10 9 8 7 6 5 4 3 2 1

Printed in the United States of America

For Dave, Terri,
and Captain Bolshevik

Introduction

In the summer of 1956 I was eighteen years old and living in New York for the first time. (I had come here two or three times previously on three-day trips with my parents, but this was different.) I had just finished my freshman year at Antioch College, and I was going to spend the months of August through October at a job arranged through the college's cooperative education department. I planned to be a writer, and the job chosen for me was as a mail clerk at Pines Publications, on East 40th Street. Pines had a paperback line, Popular Library, as well as a slew of comic books and magazines, including a couple of still-surviving pulps, like *Ranch Romances*.

With two roommates, I moved first to a rooming house at 147 West 14th, then to another at 108 West Twelfth, and finally to an actual apartment at 54 Barrow Street. All of these addresses are in Greenwich Village, and that's where I spent all the time I didn't spend at Pines Publications. On Sunday afternoons I joined the crowd singing folk songs around the fountain in Washington Square, and when the cops chased everybody out of there at six in the evening, we all went back to Barrow Street and kept the party going for as long as the neighbors could stand it.

I met a remarkable array of people. The political spectrum included the usual range of lefties, but there were also some exotic strains. I recall Welsh nationalists, Basque separatists, and Catholic anarchists. All of us had our pictures taken time and time again by FBI agents in suits who showed up every Sunday with their cameras.

I went back to Antioch in November, but the die was cast. The following summer I came back to the city and found myself a job at a literary agency. I had already sold my first story, and by the end of the year I'd sold a bunch more and written a novel. I'd also dropped out of school. I went back after a year but it didn't take; I kept cutting my classes and writing all night. So I dropped out again and moved to

New York and got drunk and moved back to Buffalo and opened a jazz club and got married and moved to New York again. We lived on West 69th Street and then on Central Park West. I was writing softcore paperback novels, fifteen or more of them a year, and I'd published a couple of crime novels under my own name, including *Mona* and *Coward's Kiss*. My wife got pregnant and my father died and my daughter was born and we moved back to a suburb of Buffalo. It seemed like a good idea at the time.

Then one day I was reading a long article on sleep in *Time* magazine. There was some interesting stuff on experiments in sleep deprivation and dream deprivation, and almost as an afterthought it mentioned that there were a few cases on record of human beings who seemed to exist without any sleep whatsoever.

I thought that was pretty interesting.

And it struck me that a character whose cerebral sleep center had been damaged would be interesting to write about.

Not long thereafter, I was looking for something in the *Encyclopaedia Britannica* and found something else instead. What I found was the fascinating fact that a Stuart pretender to the British throne still existed. The House of Stuart ceased to rule when George I followed Anne to the throne in 1714. There was the Old Pretender, James, and the Young Pretender, Bonnie Prince Charlie, but after the latter's supporters were routed at the Battle of Culloden in 1745, the Stuart cause was pretty much a dead issue.

But now it appeared that there was some little German princeling who was indeed the Stuart claimant to the throne.

Suppose this guy of mine, his sleep center destroyed by, say, a stray piece of shrapnel, suppose he was a creative lunatic in the manner of some of the people I'd met in the Village. And suppose his particular passion was to rout the Hanoverian usurpers and restore the House of Stuart to the English monarchy. . . .

Thinking about it, I began to get some sense of the guy. With all that wide-awake time on his hands, he could do all the things we all say we'd do if we only had time enough. Like learn a foreign language and keep up on our correspondence and study things just for the fun of it. And he could make ends meet by writing theses for people and term papers for them, and taking their exams for them, too.

So I was beginning to know a lot about Tanner (although I hadn't picked a name for him yet). But I didn't have a story, so I couldn't sit down and start writing.

Then we moved to Wisconsin.

I had become interested in coin collecting, and had done a few freelance articles for several numismatic publications. One of them, the Whitman Numismatic Journal, was published by Western Printing, in Racine, Wisconsin. The coin supply division made those blue folders you stick coins in, and books to tell you what they're worth, and so on. They offered me a job and I took it.

One day, after I'd been in Racine a little more than a year and knew I wouldn't be staying too much longer, a fellow named Bill Higgie showed up at the office. He had lived in Racine, and had worked at Whitman for a while. Then he'd moved to Istanbul, where he'd earned an extremely precarious living for several years smuggling ancient coins and antiquities out of the country for sale to museums and collectors.

I invited him home for dinner and we stayed up until three in the morning drinking Irish whiskey and swapping stories. The stories were mostly his, since I hadn't done anything. One of the stories he told was of the treasure of the Armenian community of Smyrna, a great hoard of gold coins secreted beneath the front porch of a house in Balakesir. Along with a couple of hotshots from Aramco, he had tracked the legend to its source, found the very house in question, broke into the place where the gold had been cached, and found that someone else had beaten them to it.

Now here's the amazing part—when I woke up the next morning, mouth dry and head throbbing, I actually remembered the conversation!

I even knew what to do with it. Here, by God, was something for Tanner to do. He wouldn't be allied solely with the movement to restore the House of Stuart. No, he'd be a partisan of no end of lost causes and irredentist movements, able to communicate with all his fellows in all their native languages. And, learning of the long-lost treasure of Balakesir, he'd do what he could to liberate it.

And nobody'd beat him to it, either. Not if I was writing it.

LAWRENCE BLOCK
Greenwich Village
Fall 1993

1

The Turks have dreary jails. Or is that conjecture? The plural might be inaccurate, for all I truly knew, there might be but one jail in all of Turkey. Or there could be others, but they need not be dreary places at all. I sketched them mentally, a bevy of Turkish Delights bedecked with minarets, their floors and walls sparkling with embedded rubies, their dazzling halls patrolled by undraped Turkish maidens, and even the bars on the windows lovingly polished to a glowing sheen.

But, whatever the case, there was at least one dreary jail in Turkey. It was in Istanbul, it was dank and dirty and desolate, and I was in it. The floor of my cell could have been covered by a nine-by-twelve rug, but that would have hidden the decades of filth that had left their stamp upon the wooden floor. There was one small barred window, too small to let very much air in or out, too high to afford more than a glimpse of the sky. When the window turned dark, it was presumably night; when it grew blue again, I guessed that morning had come. But, of course, I could not be certain that the window even opened to the outside. For all I knew, some idiot Turk alternately lit and extinguished a lamp outside that window to provide me with this illusion.

A single twenty-five-watt bulb hung from the ceiling and kept my cell the same shade of gray day and night. I'd been provided with a sagging army cot and a folding cardtable chair. There was a chamber pot in one corner of my chamber. The cell door was a simple affair of vertical bars, through which I could see a bank of empty cells opposite. I never saw another prisoner, never heard a human sound except for the Turkish guard who seemed to be assigned to me. He came morning, noon, and night with food. Breakfast was always a slab of cold black toast and a cup of thick black coffee. Lunch and dinner were always the same—a tin plate piled with a suspicious pilaff, mostly rice with occasional bits of lamb and shreds of vegetable matter of indeterminate origin. Incredibly enough, the pilaff was delicious. I lived in constant fear that misguided humanitarian impulses might lead my captors to vary my monotonous diet, substituting something inedible for the blessed pilaf. But twice a day my guard brought pilaff, and twice a day I wolfed it down.

It was the boredom that was stifling. I had been arrested on a Tuesday. I'd flown to Istanbul from Athens, arriving around ten in the morning, and I knew something had gone wrong when the customs officer took far too much time pawing through my suitcase. When he sighed at last and closed the bag, I said, "Are you quite through?"

"Yes. You are Evan Tanner?"

"Yes."

"Evan Michael Tanner?"

"Yes."

"American?"

"Yes."

2

"You flew from New York to London, from London to Athens, and from Athens to Istanbul?"

"Yes."

"You have business in Istanbul?"

"Yes."

He smiled. "You are under arrest," he said.

"Why?"

"I am sorry," he said, "but I am not at liberty to say."

My crime seemed destined to remain a secret forever. Three uniformed Turks drove me to jail in a jeep. A clerk took my watch, my belt, my passport, my suitcase, my necktie, my shoelaces, my pocket comb and my wallet. He wanted my ring, but it wouldn't leave my finger, so he let me keep it. My uniformed bodyguard led me down a flight of stairs, through a catacombic maze of corridors, and ushered me into a cell.

There was nothing much to do in that cell. I don't sleep, have not slept in sixteen years—more of that later— so I had the special joy of being bored, not sixteen hours a day, like the normal prisoner, but a full twenty-four. I ached for something to read, anything at all. Wednesday night I asked my guard if he could bring me some books or magazines.

"I don't speak English," he said in Turkish.

I *do* speak Turkish, but I thought it might be worth-while to keep this a secret. "Just a book or a magazine," I said in English. "Even an old newspaper."

In Turkish he said, "Your mother loves to perform fellatio upon syphilitic dogs."

I took the proffered plate of pilaff. "Your fly is open," I said in English.

He looked down immediately. His fly was not open, and his eyes focused reproachfully on me, "I don't speak English," he said again in Turkish. "Your mother spreads herself for camels."

3

Dogs, camels. He went away, and I ate the pilaff and wondered what had led them to arrest me, and precisely why they were holding me, and if they would ever let me go. My guard pretended he could not speak English, and I feigned ignorance of Turkish. The high window turned alternately blue and black, the guard brought toast and pilaff and pilaff, toast and pilaff and pilaff, toast and pilaff and pilaff. The chamber pot began to approach capacity, and I amused myself by calculating just when it would overflow and by trying to imagine how I might bring this to the attention of a guard who refused to admit to a knowledge of English. Would either of us lose face if we talked in French?

The pattern changed, finally, on my ninth day in jail, a Wednesday. I thought it was Tuesday—I'd lost a day somewhere—but it turned out that I was wrong. I had my usual breakfast, paid my usual tribute to my chamber pot, and performed a brief regimen of setting-up exercises. An hour or so after breakfast I heard footsteps in the hallway. My guard unlocked my door, and two uniformed men came into my cell. One was very tall, very thin, very much the officer. The other was shorter, fatter, sweaty, and moustached, and possessed an abundance of gold teeth.

Both carried clipboards and wore sidearms. The tall one studied his clipboard for a moment, then looked at me. "You are Evan Tanner," he said.

"Yes."

He smiled. "I believe we will be able to release you very shortly, Mr. Tanner," he said. "I regret the need to have dealt so unpleasantly with you, but I'm sure you can understand."

"No, I can't, frankly."

He studied me. "Why, there were so many points to be checked, and naturally it was necessary to keep you in a safe place while these checks were made. And then you acted in such a strange manner, you know. You never questioned your confinement, you never banged furiously on the bars of your cell, you never slept—"

"I don't sleep."

"But we did not know that then, don't you see?" he smiled again. "You did not demand to see the American ambassador. Every American invariably demands to see the ambassador. If an American is overcharged in a restaurant, he wants to bring the matter at once to his ambassador's attention. But you seemed to accept everything—"

I said, "When rape is inevitable, lie back and enjoy it."

"What? Oh, I see. But that is a sophisticated reaction, you understand, and it called for explanation. We contacted Washington and learned quite a great deal about you. Not everything, I am quite certain, but a great deal." He looked around the cell. "Perhaps you've tired of your surroundings. Let us find more comfortable quarters. I must ask you several questions, and then you will be free to go."

We left the cell. The short man with the gold teeth led the way, my interrogator and I followed side by side, and my guard trailed along a few paces behind. Walking was awkward. I'd evidently lost a little weight, and my beltless pants had to be held up manually. My shoes, lacking laces, kept slipping off my feet.

In an airy cleaner room a floor above, the taller man sat beneath a flattering portrait of Ataturk and smiled benevolently at me. He asked if I knew why they had arrested me so promptly. I said that I did not.

"Would you care to know?"

"Of course."

"You are a member"—he consulted the clipboard—"of a fascinating array of organizations, Mr. Tanner. We did not know just how many causes had caught your interest, but when your name appeared on the incoming passenger list it did line up with our membership rosters for two rather interesting organizations. You belong, it would seem, to the Pan-Hellenic Friendship Society. True?"

"Yes."

"And to the League for the Restoration of Cilician Armenia?"

"Yes."

He stroked his chin. "Neither of these two organizations is particularly friendly to Turkish interests, Mr. Tanner. Each is composed of a scattering of—how would you say it? Fanatics? Yes, fanatics. The Pan-Hellenic Friendship Society has been extremely vocal lately. We suspect they're peripherally involved in some acts of minor terrorism over Cyprus. The Armenian fanatics have been dormant since the close of the war. Most people would probably be surprised to know that they even exist, and we've had no trouble from them for a very long time. But suddenly you appear in Istanbul and are recognized as a member of not one but both of these organizations." He paused significantly. "It might interest you to know that our records indicate you are the only man on earth to hold membership in both organizations."

"Is that so?"

"Yes."

"That's very interesting," I said.

He offered me a cigarette. I declined. He took one himself and lit it. The smell of Turkish tobacco was overpowering.

"Would you care to explain these memberships, Mr. Tanner?"

I thought this over. "I'm a joiner," I said finally.

"Yes, I'm sure you are."

"I'm a member of... many groups."

"Indeed." He referred to the clipboard once more. "Our list may not be complete, but you may fill in any significant omissions. You belong to the two groups I mentioned. You also belong to the Irish Republican Brotherhood and the Clann-na-Gaille. You are a member of the Flat Earth Society of England, the Macedonian Friendship League, the Industrial Workers of the World, the Libertarian League, the Society for a Free Croatia, the Confederación Nacional del Trabajadores de España, the Committee Allied Against Fluoridation, the Serbian Brotherhood, the Nazdóya Fedèróvka, and the Lithuanian Army-in-Exile." He looked up and sighed. "This list goes on and on. Need I read more?"

"I'm impressed with your research."

"A simple call to Washington, Mr. Tanner. They have a lengthy file on you, did you know that?"

"Yes."

"Why on earth do you belong to all these groups? According to Washington, you don't seem to *do* anything. You attend an occasional meeting, you receive an extraordinary quantity of pamphlets, you associate with subversives of every conceivable persuasion, but you don't do much of anything. Can you explain yourself?"

"Lost causes interest me."

"Pardon?"

It seemed pointless to explain it to him, as pointless as the many sessions I'd had with FBI agents over the years. The charm of an organization devoted to a singularly hopeless cause is evidently lost on the average person and certainly on the average bureaucrat or policeman. One either appreciates the beauty of a band of three hundred men scattered across the face of the earth with nothing more on their mind, say, than the utterly unattainable dream of separating Wales from the United Kingdom—one either finds this heartrendingly marvelous or dismisses the little band as a batch of nuts and cranks.

But, however futile my explanation, I knew that a slew of words of any sort would be better in this Turk's eyes than my silence. I talked, and he listened and stared at me, and when I finished he sat silent for a moment and then shook his head.

"You astound me," he said.

There seemed no need for a reply.

"It seemed quite obvious to us that you were an *agent provocateur*. We contacted your American Central Intelligence Agency, and they denied any knowledge of you, which made us all the more certain you were one of their agents. We're still not certain that you're not. But you don't fit any of the standard molds. You don't make any sense."

"That's true," I said.

"You don't sleep. You're thirty-four years old and lost the power to sleep when you were eighteen. Is that correct?"

"Yes."

"In the war?"

"Korea."

"Turkey sent troops to Korea," he said.

This was indisputably true, but it seemed a conversational dead end. This time I decided to wait him out. He put out his cigarette and shook his head sadly at me.

"You were shot through the head? Is that what happened?"

8

"More or less. A piece of shrapnel. Nothing seemed damaged—it was just a fleck of shrapnel, actually—so they patched me up and gave me my gun and sent me back into battle. Then I just wasn't sleeping, not at all. I didn't know why. They thought it was mental—something like that. The trauma of being wounded. It was nothing like that because the wound hadn't shaken me up much at all. I never knew I was hit at the time, not until someone noticed I was bleeding a little from the forehead, so there wasn't any trauma involved. Then they—"

"What is trauma?"

"Shock."

"I see. Continue."

"Well, they kept knocking me out with shots, and I would stay out until the shot wore off and then wake up again. They couldn't even induce normal sleep. They decided finally that the sleep center of my brain was destroyed. They're not sure just what the sleep center is or just how it works, but evidently I don't have one any more. So I don't sleep."

"Not at all?"

"Not at all."

"Don't you become tired?"

"Of course. I rest when I'm tired. Or switch from a mental activity to a physical one, or vice versa."

"But you can just go on and on without sleep?"

"Yes."

"That is incredible."

It isn't, of course. Science still doesn't know what makes men sleep, or how, or why. Men will die without it. If you keep a man forcibly awake, he will die sooner than if you starve him. And yet, no one knows what sleep does for the body or how it comes on a person.

"You are in good health, Mr. Tanner?"

9

"Yes."

"Is it not a strain on your heart, this endless wakefulness?"

"It doesn't seem to be."

"And you'll live as long as anyone else?"

"Not quite as long, according to the doctors. Their statistics indicate that I'll live three-fourths of my natural life span, barring accidents, of course. But I don't trust their figures. The condition just doesn't occur often enough to afford any conclusions."

"But they say you won't live as long."

"Yes. Though my insomnia probably won't cut off as many years from my life as would smoking, for example."

He frowned. He'd just lit a fresh cigarette and didn't enjoy being reminded of its ill effects. So he changed the subject.

"How do you live?" he asked.

"From day to day."

"You misunderstand me. How do you earn your living?"

"I receive a disability pension from the Army. For my loss of sleep."

"They pay you one hundred twelve dollars per month. Is that correct?"

It was. I've no idea how the Defense Department had arrived at that sum. I'm certain there's no precedent.

"You do not live on one hundred twelve dollars per month. What else do you do? You are not employed, are you?"

"Self-employed."

"How?"

"I write doctoral dissertations and master's theses."

"I do not understand."

"I write theses and term papers for students. They turn

10

them in as their own work. Occasionally I take examinations for them as well—at Columbia or New York University."

"Is this allowed?"

"No."

"I see. You help them cheat?"

"I help them compensate for their personal inadequacies."

"There is a name for this profession? It is a recognized profession?"

The hell with him, I decided. The hell with him and his questions and his rotten jail. "I'm called a stentaphator," I explained. He had me spell it and he wrote it down very carefully. "Stentaphators are subsidiary scholars concerned with suasion and ambidexterity."

He didn't know *trauma;* I was fairly sure *suasion* and *ambidexterity* would ring no bells, and I guessed he wouldn't ask for definitions. His English was excellent, his accent only slight. The only weapon in my arsenal was double-talk.

He lit still another cigarette—the man was going to smoke himself sick—and narrowed his eyes at me. "Why are you in Turkey, Mr. Tanner?"

"I'm a tourist."

"Don't be absurd. You've never left the United States since Korea, according to Washington. You applied for a passport less than three months ago. You came at once to Istanbul. Why?"

I hesitated.

"For whom are you spying, Mr. Tanner? The CIA? One of your little organizations? Tell me."

"I'm not spying at all."

"Then why are you here?"

I hesitated. Then I said, "There is a man in Antakya who makes counterfeit gold coins. He's noted for his

11

counterfeit Armenian pieces, but he does other work as well. Marvelous work. According to Turkish law, he's able to do this with impunity. He never counterfeits Turkish coins, so it's all perfectly legal."

"Continue."

"I plan to see him, buy an assortment of coins, smuggle them back into the United States, and sell them as genuine."

"It is a violation of Turkish law to remove antiquities from the country."

"These are not antiquities. The man makes them himself. I intended to have him give me an affidavit testifying that the coins were forgeries. It's a violation of U.S. law to bring gold into the country in any form, and it's a case of fraud to sell a counterfeit coin as genuine, but I was prepared to take that chance." I smiled. "I had no intention, though, of violating Turkish law. You may believe me."

The man looked at me for a long time. Finally he said, "That is an extraordinary explanation."

"It happens to be true."

"You sat for nine days in jail with an explanation in your pocket that would have gotten you released at once. That argues for its truth, does it not? Otherwise you might have told your cover story right away, accompanied it with a bribe, and attempted to get out of our hands the very first day; before we began to learn so many interesting things about you. A counterfeiter in Antakya. Armenian gold coins, for the love of God. When did Armenians make gold coins?"

"In the Middle Ages."

"One moment, please." He used a phone on his desk and called someone. I looked up at Ataturk's portrait and listened to his conversation. He was asking some bureaucrat somewhere if there was in fact a counterfeiter in Antakya and what sort of things the man produced. He was not overly surprised to find out that my story checked out.

To me he said, "If you are lying, you have built your lie on true foundations. I find it frankly inconceivable that you would travel to Istanbul for such a purpose. There is a profit in it?"

"I could buy a thousand dollars worth of rare forgeries and sell them for thirty thousand dollars by passing them as genuine."

"Is that true?"

"Yes."

He was silent for a moment. "I still do not believe you," he said at length. "You are a spy or a saboteur of one sort or another. I am convinced of it. But it makes no matter. Whatever you are, whatever your intentions, you must leave Turkey. You are unwelcome in our country, and there are men in your own country who are very much interested in speaking with you.

"Mustafa will see that you get a bath and a chance to change your clothes. At three-fifteen this afternoon you will board a Pan American flight for Shannon Airport. Mustafa will be with you. You will have two hours between planes and you will then board another Pan American flight for Washington, where Mustafa will turn you over to agents of your own government." Mustafa, who was to do all this, was the grubby little man who had brought my pilaff twice a day and my toast each morning. If he was important enough to accompany me to Washington, then he was a rather high-level type to use as a prison guard, which meant that I was probably thought to be the greatest threat on earth to the peace and security of the Republic of Turkey.

"We will not see you again," he went on. "I do not doubt that the United States Government will revoke your passport. Unless you are, in fact, their agent, which is still quite possible. I am beyond caring. Nothing you tell me makes any sense, and everything is probably a lie. I believe nothing that anyone tells me in this day and age."

"It's the safest course," I assured him.

"In any case, you will never return to Turkey. You are *persona non grata* here. You will leave, taking with you all of the personal belongings you brought in with you. You will leave and you will not return for any reason."

"That suits me."

"I hoped it would." He stood up, dismissing me, and Mustafa led me toward the door.

"A moment—"

I turned.

"Tell me one thing," he said. "Precisely what is the Flat Earth Society of England?"

"It's worldwide, really. Not limited to England, although it was organized there and has most of its members there."

"But what is it?"

"A group of people who believe the earth is flat, rather than round. The society is devoted to propagating this belief and winning converts to this way of thinking."

He stared at me. I stared back.

"Flat," he said. "Are these people crazy?"

"No more than you or I."

I left him with that to contemplate. Mustafa led me to a rudimentary bathroom and stood outside while I washed an impressive amount of filth from my body. When I got out of the shower he handed me my suitcase. I put on clean clothes and closed my suitcase. I tied my dirty clothing into a fetid bundle—shoes and socks and all—

and passed the reeking mess to Mustafa. He was not an overly clean man himself, but he took a step backward at once.

"In the name of peace and friendship and the International Brotherhood of Stentaphators, I present this clothing as a gift and tribute unto the great Republic of Turkey."

"I don't speak English," Mustafa lied.

"What the hell does that mean?" I demanded. "Oh, the devil with you."

We stopped at the clerk's desk. I was given back my belt, my necktie, my shoelaces, my pocket comb, my wallet, and my watch. Mustafa took my passport and tucked it away in a pocket. I asked him for it, and he grinned and told me he didn't speak English.

We left the building. The sun was absolutely blinding. My eyes were unequal to it. I wondered if Mustafa would consider dropping his pose of not speaking English. We would have a long flight together. Would he want to pass the whole trip in stony silence?

I decided that I could probably get him to talk, but that it might be better if I didn't. A silent Mustafa could well be more bearable than a talkative one, especially since I would be able to pick up some paperbacks to read on the plane. And I did seem to have an advantage. He spoke English and didn't know I knew it. I spoke Turkish, and he didn't know that, either. Why give up that sort of edge?

We walked along toward a 1953 Chevrolet, its fenders crippled, its body riddled with rust. We sat in back, and Mustafa told the driver to take us to the airport. He leaned forward, and I heard him tell the driver that I was a very deceptive spy from the United States of America and that I was emphatically not to be trusted.

They all see too many James Bond movies. They

15

expect spies everywhere and overlook the profit motive entirely. A spy? It was the last thing on earth I would ever become. I had no intentions of spying for or against Turkey or anyone else.

I had come, quite simply, so that I could steal approximately three million dollars in gold.

2

It had begun some months before in Manhattan at the junction of three streams—a job, a girl, and a most noble lost cause. The job involved preparation of a thesis that would win Brian Cudahy a master's degree in history from Columbia University. The girl was Kitty Bazerian, who rolls her belly in Chelsea nightclubs as Alexandra the Great. The noble lost cause, one of the noblest, one of the most utterly lost, was the League for the Restoration of Cilician Armenia.

I first saw Brian Cudahy on a Saturday morning. My mail had just arrived, and I was sitting in my living room sorting it. I receive a tremendous amount of mail. I'm on hundreds of mailing lists and I subscribe to a great many periodicals, and my mail carrier detests me. I live on 107th Street a few doors west of Broadway. My neighbors are transients and addicts and students and Orientals and actors and harlots, six classes of people who get little in the way of mail. Bills from Con Ed and the telephone company, slingers from the supermarkets, quarterly messages from their congressman, little else. I, on the other hand, burden my mailman with a sack of paper garbage every day.

My bell rang. I pressed a buzzer to admit my caller into the building. He climbed four flights of stairs and hesitated in the hallway. I waited, and he knocked, and I opened the door.

"Tanner?"

"Yes."

"I'm Brian Cudahy. I called you last night—"

"Oh, yes," I said. "Come in." He seated himself in the rocking chair. "Coffee?"

"If it's no trouble."

I made instant coffee in the kitchen and brought back two cups. He was looking all over the apartment. I suppose it's a little unusual. People have said that it looks more like a library than an apartment. There are four rooms besides the kitchen and the bath, and in each room the walls are done in floor-to-ceiling bookcases, almost all of which are full. Beyond that, there's rather little in the way of furniture. I've a large bed in one room, a very large writing desk in another, a few chairs scattered here and there, and a small dresser in still another room, and that's about all. I don't find the place unusual at all, myself. When one is a compulsive reader and researcher and when one has a full twenty-four hours a day at his disposal, not having to allot eight for sleep and eight for work, one certainly ought to have plenty of books on hand.

"Is the coffee all right?"

"Oh!" He looked up, startled. "Yes, of course. I...uh...I'm going to need your help. Mr. Tanner."

He was about twenty-four, I guessed. Clean-cut, bright-faced, short-haired, with an air of incipient success about

18

him. He looked like a student but not at all like a scholar. An increasing number of such persons pursue graduate degrees these days. Industry considers a bachelor's degree indispensable and, by a curious extension, regards master's degrees and doctorates as a way of separating the men from the boys. I don't understand this. Why should a Ph.D. awarded for an extended essay on color symbolism in the poetry of Pushkin have anything to do with a man's competence to develop a sales promotion campaign for a manufacturer of ladies' underwear?

"My thesis is due the middle of next month," Cudahy was saying. "I can't seem to get anywhere on it. And I heard that you . . . you were recommended as—"

"As one who writes theses?"

He nodded.

"What's your field?" I asked.

"History."

"You've a topic already assigned, of course."

"Yes."

"What is it?"

He swallowed. "Sort of offbeat, I'm afraid."

"Good."

"Excuse me?"

"Offbeat topics are the best. What's yours?"

"The Turkish persecutions of Armenians during the late nineteenth century and immediately before and after the First World War." He grinned. "Don't ask me how I got saddled with that one. I can't figure it out, myself. Do you know anything about the subject, Mr. Tanner?"

"Yes."

"You do?" He was incredulous. "Honestly?"

"I know a great deal about it," I said.

"Then can you . . . uh . . . write the thesis?"

"Probably. Have you done anything on it to date?"

"I have notes here—"

"Notes that you've shown an instructor or just your own work?"

"No one's seen anything yet. I've had some oral conferences with my instructor but nothing very important."

I waved his briefcase aside. "Then I'd rather not see your notes," I told him. "I find it easier to start fresh if you don't mind."

"You'll do it?"

"For seven hundred fifty dollars."

His face clouded. "That seems high. I don't—"

"A master's degree is worth an extra fifteen hundred to industry the first year. That's minimal. I'm charging you half your first year's differential. If you try to haggle, the price goes up, not down."

"It's a deal."

"This is for Columbia, you said?"

"Yes."

"And your grades have been—"

"B average."

"All right. About a hundred-page thesis? And you want it the middle of next month?"

"Yes."

"You'll have it. Call me in three weeks, and I'll let you know how it's coming along."

"Three weeks."

"Don't call before then. And I'll want half the money now, if it's all the same to you."

"I don't have it on me. Can I bring it this afternoon?"

"You do that," I said.

He was back at two that afternoon with $375 in cash. He was just a little reluctant to part with it—I don't think because he would miss the money so much but because this made the deal firm, committed him to a plan that he knew very well was morally reprehensible. He was purchasing his master's degree. It would be a big status thing for him, that master's, and he'd have gotten it unfairly, and it would always bother him a little, and he knew as much already. But he handed me the money, and I took it, and we both sealed our pact with the devil.

"I suppose you've done lots of theses," he said.

"Quite a number."

"Many in history?"

"Yes. And a good number in English, and a few in sociology and economics. And some other things."

"What did you do your own on?"

"My own?"

"Your master's and doctorate."

"I don't even have a bachelor's," I told him truthfully. "I joined the Army the day I left high school. Korea. I never did go to college."

He found this extraordinary. He talked about how easy it would be for me to go through college and walk off with highest honors. "It would be a snap for you. Why, you could write your thesis with no sweat. The exams, the whole routine. It would be nothing for you."

"Exactly," I said.

Cudahy's thesis was a very simple matter. I already knew quite a good deal about the Terrible Turk and the Starving Armenians. My library contained all the basic texts on the subject and more than a few lesser-known works, including several in Armenian. I speak Armenian, but reading it is a chore. The alphabet is unfamiliar and the construction tedious. I also had an almost complete file of the publications in English of the League for the Restoration of Cilician Armenia. Biased though they were, the League's pamphlets could not fail to impress in a bibliography.

It was pleasant work. Research is a joy, especially when one is not burdened with an excessive reverence for the truth. By inventing an occasional source and injecting an occasional spurious footnote, one softens the harsh curves in the royal road of scholarship. I studied, I ate, I worked out at the 110th Street Gym, I read, I kept up my correspondence, and I developed Cudahy's thesis with little difficulty.

I narrowed his topic somewhat, focusing on the Armenian Nationalist movements that had in large part provoked the Turkish massacres. Hunchak and Daschnak, organized in 1885 and 1890 respectively, had worked to develop a national consciousness and pressed for liberation from the Ottoman Empire. The minor Kurdish massacre of 1894 led to an absorbing parade of Big Power manipulations and was followed a year later by Abdu-l-Hamid's mammoth slaughter of eighty thousand Armenians.

But it was during World War I, when Turkey fought on the Axis side and feared her Armenian subjects as a potential fifth column, that the Armenian massacres reached their height and the phrase "Starving Armenians" found its way into our language. In mid-1915 the Turks went berserk. In one community after another the Armenian population was uprooted, men and women and children were massacred indiscriminately, and those who were not put to the sword either fled the country or quietly starved.

After the war the Soviets took Armenia proper, establishing an Armenian Soviet Socialist Republic. The areas that remained Turkish had largely lost their Armenian population. The last large concentration of Armenians to suffer en masse were those in the city of Smyrna, now Izmir. The Greeks seized the town in the Greco-Turkish War that followed close upon the signing of the armistice. When Ataturk recaptured Smyrna, the city was burned, and the Greeks and Armenians were systematically destroyed. An earthquake further reduced the city in 1928, but by that time there were few Armenians left in it.

Smyrna, then, was an afterthought, a sort of footnote to the whole business. My main focus was on the Nationalist movements, their organization, their development, their aims, and their ultimate effects. I expected to finish the thesis well ahead of schedule and I expected to go no further with the study of the destruction of Smyrna. But I had not then met Kitty or her grandmother.

Kitty and I met at a wedding in the Village. My friend Owen Morgan was being married to a Jewish girl from White Plains. Owen is a Welsh poet with no discernible talent who had discovered that one could make a fair living by drinking an impressive amount, spouting occasional poetry, seducing every comely female within reach, and generally behaving like the shade of Dylan Thomas. He startled me by asking me to be his best man, an office I had never before performed. So I stood up for him in a drab loft on Sullivan Street at the ceremony performed by a priest friendly to the Catholic Workers. Neither of them was Catholic, but Owen had lived at the CW settlement on Christie Street for a few months before he discovered the potential of the Dylan Thomas bit. (I'm a member of the Catholic Workers myself, although I don't give them as much of my time as I probably should. They're a wonderful organization.) I stood up for Owen and passed him the ring at the appropriate time, and afterward Kitty Bazerian danced at his wedding.

She was small and slender and dark, with fine black hair and huge brown eyes. She stood demurely, garbed

23

in a wisp of diaphanous fluff, and someone said, "Now Kitty Bazerian will dance for us," and the house band from the New Life Restaurant began to play, and her body sang in the center of the improvised stage, music in motion, silk, velvet, perfection, adding a wholly new dimension to sensuality.

Afterward I found her at the bar, dressed now in skirt and sweater and black tights, which was about right for Owen's wedding.

"Alexandra the Great," I said.

"Who told you? They promised not to say."

"I recognized you myself."

"Honestly?"

"I've watched you dance at the New Life. And at the Port Said before that."

"And you recognized me right away?"

"Of course. I never knew that Alexandra the Great was an Armenian."

"A starving Armenian right about now. Aren't they having anything to eat?"

"It would spoil Owen's image."

"I suppose we have to respect his image. But I already had too much to drink and I'm starving."

"May it never be said that Evan Tanner let an Armenian starve. Why don't we get out of here?"

We did. I suggested the Sayat Nova at Bleecker and Charles. She asked me why I was so very hipped on Armenians. I told her I was writing a thesis on Armenia.

"You're a student?"

"No, I'm just writing a thesis."

"I don't . . . wait a minute, you're Evan *Tanner!* Sure, Owen told me about you. He says you're crazier than he is."

"He may be right."

"And you're writing about Armenians now? You ought

24

to meet my grandmother. She could tell you all about how we lost the family fortunes. She makes a good story out of it. According to her, we were the richest Armenians in Turkey. Gold coins, she says; more gold coins than you could count. And now the Turks have it all." She laughed. "Isn't that always the way? Owen insists he's a direct descendant of Owen Glendower and the rightful King of all of Wales. The Sayat Nova sounds fine, Evan. But I warn you, I'm going to be expensive. I'll eat everything they've got."

I don't remember what we had or how it tasted. There was a good red wine with the meal, but we got drunker on each other than on anything else. It does not happen often for me, the special magic, the perfect harmony. It happened this time.

She talked some about her dancing. I was delighted to discover that she had no higher ambitions. She did not want to become a ballerina, or get a guest shot on the Sullivan show, or found a new school of modern dance. She just wanted to go on dancing at the New Life for as long as they wanted her.

I, on the other hand, have many ambitions and I told her of them. "Someday," I confided, "we'll restore the House of Stuart to the English throne. The Jacobite movement has never entirely died out, you know. There are men in the Scottish Highlands who would rise at any moment to throw out those Hanoverian interlopers."

"You're putting me on—"

"Oh, no," I said, wagging a finger at her. "The last reigning Stuart was Anne. She died in 1714 and they brought over a Hanoverian, a German. George I. And ever since that day the Germans have sat upon the English throne. If you think about it, it's an outrage."

"But the House of Stuart—"

"There have been attempts," I said. "Bonnie Prince

25

Charlie in 1745. All of Scotland rose to support him, but the French didn't do all they were supposed to do, and nothing came of it. The English won the Battle of Culloden Moor and thought that was the end of it." I paused significantly. "But they were wrong."

"They were?"

"The House of Stuart has not died out, Kitty. There has always been a Stuart Pretender to the English throne, although some of them have worked harder at it than others. The current Pretender is Rupert. Someday he'll reign as Rupert I, after Betty Saxe-Coburg and her German court have been routed."

"Betty Saxe-Coburg . . . oh, Elizabeth, of course. And who is Rupert?"

"He's a Bavarian crown prince."

She looked at me for a long moment and then began to laugh. "Oh, that's beautiful! That's priceless, Evan. I love it!"

"Do you?"

"Replacing the . . . the German usurpers with . . . oh, it's *great* . . . with the crown prince of *Bavaria*—"

"The true English claimant."

"I love it. Oh, sign me up, Evan. It's better than a Barbara Stanwyck movie. Oh, it's grand. I love it!"

And outside, a breeze playing with her marvelous black hair, she said, "I live with my mother and my grandmother, so that's out. Do you have a place we can go to?"

"Yes."

"But Owen said something about you not sleeping. I mean—"

"I don't, but I have a bed."

"How sweet of you," she said, taking my arm, "to have a bed."

3

It was about a week after that when I finally did meet Kitty's grandmother. Kitty had told me several times that I would enjoy the old woman's story, and she became especially enthusiastic when I showed her my membership card in the League for the Restoration of Cilician Armenia. She had never heard of the group—rather few people have, actually—but she was certain her grandmother would be delighted.

"She has some pretty grim memories," Kitty said. "She was the only one of the family to get away. The Turks killed everybody else. I have a feeling she got raped in the bargain, but she never said anything about it exactly, and it's not the kind of subject you discuss with your grandmother. If you're really interested in all this Armenian jazz, you'll enjoy her. And she's getting older, you know, and I think she may be getting a little flaky, so not many people listen to her very much any more."

"I'd love to meet her."

"Would you? She'll be all excited. She's like a kid sometimes."

Kitty lived in Brooklyn, just across the bridge, in a neighborhood that was largely Syrian and Lebanese with a scattering of Armenians. We walked from the subway. It was early afternoon. Her mother was out waiting on tables in a neighborhood diner. Her grandmother sat in front of the television set watching one of those afternoon game shows where everyone laughs and smiles all the time.

Kitty said, "Grandma, this is—"

"Wait," Grandma said. "See that lady, she just won a Pontiac convertible, can you imagine? Now she has to decide to keep it or trade it for what's behind the curtain. See, she don't know what's behind the curtain. She has to decide without looking. See!"

The woman traded. The curtain opened, and Grandma sucked in her breath, then exploded with strident laughter. Behind the curtain was a set of Teflon-coated aluminum frying pans.

"For this she trades the Pontiac convertible," Grandma said. "With four-speed transmission and power seats, can you believe it?" The woman who had made this mistake was crying bravely, and the emcee was smiling and saying something about it all being part of the game. "Ha!" said Grandma, and pressed a remote-control button to extinguish the program. "Now," she said, whirling around to face us. "Who is this? You're married, Katin?"

"No," Kitty-Katin said. "Grandma, this is Evan Tanner. He wanted to see you."

"To see me?"

She was a gnomish little woman, her still-black hair parted absurdly in the middle, a strange light dancing merrily in her brown eyes. She was smoking a Helmar cigarette and had a tall glass of a dangerous orange liquid beside her. This was her life—a chair in front of a television set in her daughter's house. It was extraordinary, her eyes said, that a young man would come to see her.

"He's a writer," Kitty explained. "He is very interested in the story of how you left Turkey. Of the riches and the massacres and...uh...all of that."

"His name?"

"Evan Tanner."

"Tanner? He is Armenian?"

In Armenian I said, "I am not Armenian myself, Mrs. Bazerian, but I have long been a great friend of the Armenian people and their supporter in their heroic fight for freedom."

Her eyes caught fire. "He speaks Armenian!" she cried. "Katin, he speaks Armenian!"

"I knew she would love you," Kitty told me.

"Katin, make coffee. Mr. Tanner and I must talk. When did you learn to speak Armenian, Mr. Tanner? My own Katin cannot speak it. Her own mother can speak it only poorly. Katin, make coffee the right way, not this powder with water spilled in it. Mr. Tanner, do you like coffee the Armenian way? If you cannot stand the spoon upright in the cup, then the coffee is too weak. We have a saying, you know, that coffee must be 'hot as hell, black as sin, and sweet as love.' But why am I speaking English with you? English I can hear on the television set. Katin, do not stand there foolishly. Make the coffee. Sit down, Mr. Tanner. Now, what shall I tell you? Eh?"

I stayed for hours. She spoke a Turkish strain of Armenian, and I had learned the language as it was spoken in the area that was now the Armenian S.S.R. So she was a bit hard to understand at first, but I caught the flavor of the dialect before long and followed her with little difficulty. She kept sending Kitty to fetch more coffee and once she chased her around the block to a bakery for baklava. She apologized for the baklava; it was Syrian, she said, and not as light and subtle as Armenian baklava. But that could not be helped, for there was no longer an Armenian baker in the neighborhood. The little rolled honey cakes were delicious, nevertheless, and Kitty made excellent coffee.

And the old woman's story was a classic. It had happened in 1922, she told me. She had been but a girl then, a girl just old enough to seek a husband. "And there were many who wanted me, Mr. Tanner. I was a pretty one then. And my father the richest man in Balikesir . . ."

Balikesir, a town about a hundred miles north of Smyrna, was the capital of Balikesir Province. She had lived there with her mother and her father and her father's father and two brothers and a sister and assorted aunts and uncles and cousins. Her father's house was one of the finest in Balikesir, and her father was the head of the town's Armenian community. A fine house it was, too, not far from the railroad station, built high upon a hill with a view for miles in all directions. A huge house, with high columns around the doorway and a sloping cement walk down to the street below. Of the five hundred Armenian families in Balikesir, none had a finer house.

"The Greeks were at war with the Turks," she told me. "Of course, we were on the side of the Greeks, and my father had raised funds for the Greeks and knew many of their leaders. There were thousands of Greeks in Balikesir, and they were good friends with the Armenians. Our churches were different, but we were all Christians, not heathens like the Turks. At first my father thought the Greeks would win. The British were going to help us, you see. But, then, no help came from the British, and my father learned that the Turks would win after all."

It was then that the gold began to come to the house in Balikesir. Every day men brought sacks of gold, she said. Some brought little leather purses, some brought suitcases, some had gold coins sewn into their garments. Each man brought the gold to her father, who counted it carefully and wrote out a receipt for it. Then the man left, and the gold was put in the basement.

"But we could not leave it there, you see. The bandits were already at the gates of Smyrna, and time was short. And my father had in his hands all the gold of all the Armenians of Smyrna."

"Of Balikesir, you mean?"

She laughed. "Of Balikesir? Oh, no. Why, there were only five hundred families of our people in Balikesir. No, they brought all the Armenian gold of Smyrna as well because they knew that Smyrna would fall first and they knew, too, that my father was a man who could be trusted. Just a few sacks would have held all the gold of Balikesir, but the riches of Smyrna—that was another matter."

Her father and his brothers had worked industriously. She recalled it all very well, she told me. One afternoon a man had come with news that Smyrna had fallen, and that very night the whole family had worked. There was a huge front porch on their house, wooden on the top, with concrete sides and front. That night her father and her uncle Poul broke through the concrete on the left side. Then the whole family carried the gold coins from the basement and hid them away beneath the porch.

They made many trips, she told me. They carried big sacks and little sacks, and once she had dropped a cloth purse, and the shiny coins had scattered all over the basement floor, and she had to scurry around picking them up and putting them back into the purse. Almost all the coins were the same, she said—a bit smaller than an American quarter, with a woman's head on one side and a man on horseback on the other, and the man, she remembered, was sticking something with a spear.

British sovereigns, of course. The head of Victoria (Vicki Hanover, *that* usurper) and the reverse was St. George slaying the dragon. That had been the most common gold coin in the Middle East, I knew; the most trusted gold piece, the coin one would choose to hoard as family or communal wealth.

At last all the coins were in place, Kitty's grandmother explained, and they filled the space beneath the porch to capacity. And then her father and her uncle mixed cement and carefully patched the opening in the concrete by the light of a single lantern. After the cement set, they rubbed little bits of gravel into it to give it an aged appearance and they dusted it with dirt from the road so it would be the same shade as the rest of the porch cement.

Until then the Turks in Balikesir had been peaceful. But now, once they had heard of Ataturk's victory a hundred miles to the south, they suddenly grew courageous. The next morning they attacked, overrunning the Greeks and Armenians. They burned the Greek quarter to the ground and they butchered every Greek and Armenian they could find. The violence in Balikesir had not made the history books. Smyrna, sacked at the same time, overshadowed it, and I don't doubt that similar massacres were taking place in enough other Turkish cities to keep Balikesir out of the limelight.

Kitty's grandmother, however, had been only in Balikesir and had seen only what took place in Balikesir. She spoke calmly of it now. The burnings, the rape, the endless murder. Children pierced with swords, old men and women shot through the back of the head—screams, gunshots, blood, death.

She was one of the few to survive, but her words

indicated that Kitty had been right: "I was young then, and pretty. And the Turks are animals. I was ravished. Can you believe this, to look at me now, that men would want to have me that way? And not just one man, no. But I was not killed. Everyone else in my family was killed, but I escaped. I was with a group of Greeks and an old Armenian man. We fled the city. We were on the roads for days. The old Armenian man died. It is funny, I cannot remember his name. We were crowded together aboard a ship. Then we were here, New York, America."

"And the gold?"

"Gone. The Turks must have it."

"Did they find it?"

"Not then, no. But they must have it now. It was years ago. And no Armenian went back for it. I was the only one of my family to live, and only the people of my family knew of the gold. So no Armenian found it, and so the Turks must have gotten it all."

Later Kitty said, "Damn you, why did you have to go and talk Armenian with her? I couldn't understand three words out of a hundred. If you think it's a picnic to sit listening to two people talk for hours and not catch a word—"

"She's a wonderful woman."

"She is, isn't she? You seemed interested in her story. Were you?"

"Very much."

"I'm glad. How on earth did you learn to speak the language, Evan? No, don't tell me. I don't even want to know. It made her whole day, though. She cornered me on the way out. Did you hear what she asked me?"

"No."

"She wanted to know if I was pregnant."

"Are you?"

"God, I hope not. I told her I wasn't, and she said I should get pregnant right away so that we would be married."

"She said that?"

"That's not all. She said you have a better chance to get pregnant if you keep your knees way up and stay that way as long as you can. She's a dirty old lady."

"She's grand."

"You're a dirty old man. Are you coming to the New Life tonight?"

"Around midnight."

"Good."

I took the subway back to my apartment and sat down at my typewriter and wrote up everything I could recall of Kitty's grandmother's story. I read through what I had written, then roamed the apartment, pulling books from the shelves, checking articles in various pamphlets and magazines. A broadside of the League for the Restoration of Cilician Armenia alluded to the confiscation of the wealth of the Armenians of Smyrna. But I could find no reference to the cache in Balikesir. Nothing at all.

A few days later the League was meeting on Attorney Street on the Lower East Side. The League meets once a month, and I go when I can. Sometimes a guest speaker discusses conditions in the Armenian Soviet Socialist Republic. Other times reports will be read from branches in other cities, other countries. Much of the time is devoted to general socializing, discussions of the rug business, gossip. As far as I know, I'm the only member who isn't Armenian. At the meeting I looked up Nezor Kalichikian, who knows everyone and everything and who, I knew, had lived in Smyrna. We drank coffee and played a game of chess which he won, as usual. I asked him about the gold of Smyrna.

"The Armenian treasure of Smyrna," he said solemnly. "What do you want to know about it?"

"What happened to it?"

He spread his small hands expressively. "What happened to everything? The Turks got it, of course. Since they could not rape it or eat it or kill it or burn it, they probably spent it. They couldn't have kept it long. They managed to rid themselves of the Armenians and the Greeks and the Jews, the only three groups in Turkey who had the slightest idea how to manage money. Yes; I know of the Armenian treasure. Are you really interested in this, Evan?"

"Yes."

"Any particular reason?"

"Some research I'm doing."

"Always research. Yes." He sipped his coffee. "The Armenians pooled their wealth, you know. It was all kept in gold. One did not keep money in paper bills in those days. Not real money, not one's savings. Always gold. The money was pooled and tucked away for safekeeping in a basement in Smyrna."

"In Smyrna?"

"Of course. And then the Turks must have taken it, because no one succeeded in getting it out of the country. The whole city was burned, you understand. The wretched Turkish quarter remained—that was the one section that might have profited by a burning—but everything else was destroyed. Ataturk's troops fired the city, and then, of course, they said that the Greeks and the Armenians had done it. Typical. I'm sure the gold was discovered during the fire. They looted everything."

"So they would have found the gold."

"Undoubtedly. If you move there, you'll lose your queen."

"Let it go, I moved it. Another game?"

35

"You resign?"

"Yes."

We set up the pieces for another game. Later he said, "There was an earthquake in Smyrna a few years after. Nineteen twenty-seven, I think."

"Nineteen twenty-eight."

"Perhaps. If the gold had not been found before, it would have been discovered then. So I'm sure the Turks have it."

"Would there have been much?"

"Oh, yes. Our people in Smyrna were quite wealthy, you know."

"And the gold was hidden right there in the city? In Smyrna?"

"Why, of course," old Nezor said. "Where else would it have been hidden?"

There were no records anywhere of the discovery of the treasure of Smyrna. It was taken for granted by everyone that the Turks had found the gold, but no one knew this for a certainty.

And there were no records anywhere to indicate that the gold had been cached in Balikesir. There was one woman's memory—and she claimed to be the only survivor who had known of the cache. Balikesir had not burned to the ground. Balikesir had not suffered an earthquake. Balikesir had suffered its private hells, but I could see a house on a hill, a porch with concrete sides and front, surviving through the years, its contents unknown and undisturbed.

That night I told Kitty. "I think it's still there, I said and explained it to her.

"Maybe it was never there in the first place. She's an old woman. She went through a big shock back then.

Who knows what she remembers? Maybe she really lived in Smyrna all the time—"

"She wouldn't get something like that wrong. Nobody forgets the name of his home town."

"I suppose not. Evan—"

"Anything could have happened," I said. "The Turks could have found it, some Armenians could have known about it and gone back for it, the new owners of the house could have remodeled and found it, but still—"

"You think it's still there."

"I think it's possible."

"Would it be very much?"

"Figure that a British sovereign is worth ten or twelve dollars today. Figure they had about half the actual volume of the hiding place filled with gold. Judging by the size of the porch as she described it and just estimating roughly, yes, it would be a lot of money."

"How much?"

"I figured it out a little while ago. I can't really estimate it—hell, I don't really know that it's there or that it was ever there in the first place."

"How much?"

"A minimum of two million dollars. Possibly twice that much. Say three million dollars, maybe."

"Three million dollars," she said.

The next morning I went downtown and applied for a passport.

4

It had all seemed magnificently simple then. I would fly to Istanbul and find some way of getting to Balikesir. I would work my way through the city—the present population is 30,000—until I found the house Kitty's grandmother had described to me. Her description was almost, but not quite, as good as a photograph. A very large house, three stories tall, on an elevation not far from the railroad station, and blessed with that extraordinary porch. There could not be too many houses of that description in Balikesir.

If I found the house, I would have to investigate to see if the porch was still intact, then provide myself with an elementary metals detector and determine if there was anything inside. And, if the gold was there, then it would be simply a matter of digging it out and taking it away. A difficult matter, no doubt, but one that could be puzzled out later.

It struck me as very likely that the gold was no longer there or had not been there in the first place. Still, one does not conclude that the grapes are sour without even attempting to see if the vine is within reach.

Three million dollars—

Just a portion of that wealth could do extraordinary things for the League for the Restoration of Cilician Armenia. Another chunk of gold would facilitate a vital worldwide direct-mail campaign for the Flat Earth Society. And more, and more. There was all that gold— perhaps—doing nothing for anyone, lying unattended and unknown, and here were all these marvelous groups able to make such good use of it.

So I had to go.

And it seemed such a facile matter, at least the first stages. I would go to Turkey and work things out from that point on. There was every reason to go and no particular reason not to. Cudahy's silly thesis was finished and would be accepted readily enough. I had completed my paper for the Jacobite Circle and mailed it off to their offices in Portree on the Isle of Skye. Most of all, I *wanted* to go. I feel that whenever possible one ought to do the things he wants to do.

How was I to know the damned Turks would arrest me?

Mustafa was poor company. He stayed with me like a summer cold and tried to shepherd me straight to the plane. I made for a newsstand and looked hungrily for something in English while Mustafa tugged at me. He could not have pried me loose with a crowbar. "Your mother was blinded by gonorrhea," I told him reasonably. "If you don't let me get something to read, I'll kill you."

The selection in English was dismal. There was a Turkish guidebook, a sort of anthropological sex manual by Margaret Mead, and four Agatha Christie mysteries. I bought everything but the Margaret Mead and let Mustafa get me onto the plane.

We sat in the tourist section. Evidently the Turkish Government intended to reroute spies as economically as possible. I had the middle seat betwen Mustafa and a fat schoolteacher—from Des Moines, I believe—who asked me at once if I was an American. I shook my head. She asked me if I spoke English, and I shook my head again. Then she put on her earphones and went to sleep.

The ride to Shannon was long, choppy, uncomfortable, and supremely dull. I was wedged between the sicksweet lavender scent of the schoolteacher and the awesome pungence of Mustafa, who evidently had never been taught to bathe. I read the Turkish guidebook— there was hardly anything in it about Balikesir—and I read the four Agatha Christies. I'd read three of them before, but it didn't really matter. After nine days in that cell I'd have read the Johannesburg phone directory and enjoyed it.

The food was good, at least. It was tasteless, naturally, but there was a fairly large piece of some sort of beef on the tray, far more meat than I had had in nine days. There were also some plastic green peas and a crunchy green and purple salad. I ate everything but found myself missing the pilaff. I might never have pilaff like that again, I thought, and then I realized how I could contrive to eat that pilaff in the future. All I had to do was go to Turkey. I would be instantly arrested and instantly jailed, and I would be fed toast and pilaff and pilaff for the rest of my life.

Except, of course, that I would never be able to return to Turkey. The Turkish Government would revoke my visa and never grant another, and the U.S. Government would probably cancel my passport. It was unfair. I had

40

done nothing. I had simply gone quietly and legally to Turkey, but they take people's passports away from them all the time. Which meant not only that I would not be able to go to Turkey again, but that I very possibly would not be able to go anywhere.

And throughout all of this there would be interrogation—endless interrogation. Why had I gone to Turkey? Who was I representing? What was I plotting? Who? What? Where? When? Why?

I have never liked being questioned. In all my sessions with the Federal Bureau of Investigation I have never enjoyed myself at all. I don't like having some competent young man sit down in my apartment and ask questions about my friends and my associations and my ideas and all of the rest.

But in each of these sessions—and there have been many of them—I have had one ultimate weapon. I have always told these officious oafs the truth. I have never lied to them. Since they cannot find any sense or logic in the way I live my life, and since I don't break their damned laws, they wind up going away and shaking their heads and clucking to themselves.

How could I tell them the truth now? How could I tell those people about the Armenian hoard?

No.

I simply could not return to the United States. I simply could not land in Washington.

I looked over at Mustafa. He had his earphones plugged into the wax in his ears and was listening, expressionless, to a medley of folk songs performed by the Norman Luboff Choir. If only there were a way of ridding myself of Mustafa, perhaps I had a chance to avoid returning to Washington. But how? Even if he dropped dead on the spot, if one of Norman Luboff's singers hit high C and burst a blood vessel in Mustafa's little brain, I was still

41

stuck on the damned airplane. How could I pry him away from me, and how could I pry myself off the flight?

Shannon—

We would be landing at Shannon. Shannon Airport in Ireland. Ireland. Not Turkey, not the United States of America. Ireland. And we would have two precious hours between planes. We would get off this plane, Mustafa and I, and we would wait in Shannon Airport for two hours before it was time to board our flight for Washington. I would have two hours to rid myself of Mustafa.

I almost shouted at the beauty of it. I knew people in Ireland! I received mail from Ireland every month; almost every week. I was an active member of the Clann-na-Gaille and the Irish Republican Brotherhood. If I could find some of those people—any of them—I was safe. They would be my sort of people, my spiritual brothers. They would hide me, they would care for me, they would *conspire* with me!

Shannon—

I closed my eyes, tried to bring the map of Ireland into focus. Dublin in the center of the extreme right, Cork at the bottom, the Six Counties of Hibernia Irredenta at the top, Galway at the left. Below Galway, Shannon Airport. And near Shannon, what? Tralee? No, that was farther down and farther to the left. Now what was the city right near Shannon?

Limerick.

Of course, Limerick. And I knew someone in Limerick. I was sure I knew someone in Limerick. Who?

Francis Geoghan and Thomas Murphy lived in Dublin. P. T. Clancy lived in Howth, which was just north of Dublin, and Padraic Fynn lived in Dun Laoghaire, which was just south of Dublin, but there was someone in Limerick, and I merely had to remember his name.

Wait, now. Dolan? Nolan? I knew it, it was coming back, it only took thinking.

It was Dolan, P. P. Dolan, Padraic Pearse Dolan, named for the greatest of the Easter Monday martyrs who had proclaimed the Irish Republic from the steps of the Post Office in O'Connell Street. And he didn't live in Limerick City but in County Limerick, and I remembered his whole address now: P. P. Dolan, Illanoloo, Croom, Co. Limerick, Republic of Ireland.

Where was Croom? It couldn't be far from Limerick itself. The whole county was not that large. If I reached him, he would hide me. He would welcome me and feed me and hide me.

If only I could get rid of Mustafa.

I looked at him, sitting contentedly while the music was piped into his ears. Dream on, I told him silently. You'll get yours, little man.

Istanbul is about 1,500 miles from Shannon. We made the trip in about three hours, and the time zones canceled out the flying time almost exactly. It had been close to four o'clock when we left Istanbul and it was about that time when we dropped through the cloud cover over Ireland.

I wasn't prepared for the greenness of it. The whole country is a brilliant green, cut up by piled-stone fences into patches of lime green and Kelly green and forest green, with thin swirling ribbons of gray road threading through the patchwork of green. There was a body of water topped with mist—the mouth of the Shannon? And there was green, miles and miles of green. I looked down at it, and something most unusual happened to me. All at once I was thinking in a rich brogue. All at once I

43

was an Irishman and a member of the Irish Republican Brotherhood. It was my own home grounds we were coming to, and Mustafa did not have a chance.

We landed, taxied, stopped. I left my five books on the plane and walked at Mustafa's side into the small one-story airport. Our luggage had been checked through to Washington, so there was no real customs check. We stood in one short line, and a pleasant young man in a green uniform checked our passports. Mustafa handed both passports to him, and the man returned them, and Mustafa took them both and pocketed them. He seemed very pleased with himself. He had my passport, after all, so where could I go?

Indeed, where *could* I go? Mustafa led me to a bench, and the two of us sat side by side upon it. I looked around. There was a door that led to the Shannon Free Shopping Center, where one could buy things at ludicrous prices before departing. I hoped Mustafa would buy himself some scented soap. There was a booth where two, beautiful, green-clad girls dispensed travel folders and sold tickets for the Bunratty Castle tour. There was a men's room. There were a pair of ticket counters for Pan Am and Aer Lingus, the Irish line. There was a ladies' room. There was a coffee bar. There was—

Of course!

I stood up. Mustafa rose to his feet at once and glared at me. "The men's room," I said. "The toilet. I have to use the toilet. I have to make a tinkle. I have to go potty, you idiot." He understood every word, of course, but we were both still pretending that he didn't. In desperation I pointed at the men's room door, then posed with my hands on my thighs and hunched forward in the classic Man Urinating posture.

"I can't go anywhere," I said. "You've got my bloody passport. Come along if you want."

And, of course, the little bastard came along.

The men's room was a long narrow affair. I walked the length of it, and my Turkish shadow stayed at my side. I paused in front of the last stall and asked him if he wanted to come in with me. He smiled and took up a position directly in front of the stall. I closed the door and bolted it.

So he thought I was James Bond, did he? Fine. Just for that I was going to *be* James Bond.

I sat down on the throne and slipped my shoes off. I shrugged out of my jacket and hung it on the peg. I placed the shoes side by side, toes pointing outward, right where they would most likely be if I were doing what I had ostensibly come to do. I hoped Mustafa would be able to see the tips of the shoes.

Then I got down on my hands and knees and looked along the floor. The floor was immaculate, incidentally, so I knew at once that I was not in Turkey. There was one stall occupied about halfway down. I waited hopefully, and a toilet flushed, and a man got to his feet and left. The outer door swung shut behind him.

Now—

I crawled under the partition, around the next toilet, under the next partition, around still another toilet, into another stall, all the way down to the end. I did this as quickly and as silently as possible, squirming on my belly like a pit viper, and certain that I was going much too slowly and making far too much noise.

I was in the very last stall when I heard the outside door open. I stopped breathing. A man came in, used the urinal, left. I wondered if Mustafa was still standing there like a soldier. I peeked out at him, and there he was, a cigarette dangling from his lower lip, his eyes focused stupidly upon my shoes.

At first I was going to slip out the door and run. But

45

how far would I get? I'd have a two-minute jump on him at the most, and I'd be running all over Ireland in my socks. No, it wouldn't do. I had to nail him and I had to get my shoes back.

I slipped out of the stall, lowered my head and charged.

He barely moved at all. At the last moment he turned lazily around just in time to see me hurtling through the air at him. His mouth fell open, and he started to take a small step backward, and I sailed into him, my head ramming him in the pit of his soft stomach, and down we went.

I was ready for a war. I had visions of us bouncing one another off plumbing fixtures, hurling karate chops at one another, fighting furiously until one of us managed to turn the tide. But this was not to be. I had never realized just how great an advantage surprise can provide. Mustafa collapsed like a blown tire. We fell in a heap, and I landed on top, and he did nothing but gape at me.

I was drunk with power. I clapped a hand over his foul mouth and leaned all my weight upon his chest and stomach. "My mother, who died some years ago, never had anything to do with dogs or camels," I said in much better Turkish than his own. "You are a foul pig to suggest such a thing." And I gave his head a tentative bang on the tile floor.

"You are also doomed." I said. "I'm a secret agent working for the establishment of a free and independent Kurdistan. I've poisoned the entire water supply of Istanbul. Within a month everyone in Turkey will perish of cholera."

His eyes rolled in his head.

"Sleep well," I said, and I slammed his head against the floor again, but infinitely harder this time. His eyes went glassy, and their lids flopped shut, and for a moment

46

I was afraid that I had actually gone and killed him. I checked his pulse. He was still alive.

I dragged him back into the stall where I'd left my shoes and jacket and I stripped off all his clothes and used strips of his shirt to tie him up and gag him. I tied his hands together behind his back and lashed his feet together and propped him up on the toilet seat. He wasn't stirring at all, and I guessed that he would stay out for quite some time. I locked the door so that no one would disturb him in the meanwhile, put on my own shoes and jacket, made a little bundle of his remaining clothing, and crawled into the adjoining compartment with it. Then I walked out of the men's room.

I took my passport and Mustafa's passport from his pants and put them both in my pocket. I stuffed his clothes in a trash can and poked them down to the bottom. I kept expecting him to emerge from the men's room and chase after me, but he stayed where he was, and I hurried through a pair of big glass doors to the outside.

No air was ever fresher. It had begun to rain, a fine misty rain, and the air had a sharp chill. My summer suit, ideal for Istanbul, was not the right thing at all for Ireland. I didn't care. I was out of Turkey and out of Mustafa's hands and free, and I could barely believe it.

There were taxis, but I didn't dare take one. Someone might remember me. I couldn't leave a trail. I asked an Aer Lingus stewardess where I could get a bus to Limerick. She pointed at an oldish double-decker bus, and I headed toward it.

"You've forgotten your luggage," she called after me.

"I'm leaving it at the airport."

I got onto the bus and went up to the top. We waited five very long minutes. Then the bus pulled out onto a narrow road and headed for Limerick. After a few moments a conductor came upstairs and collected the fare from everyone. It was five shillings. He came to me and looked at my suit and asked for seventy cents. I gave him a dollar bill, and he took a long limp ticket, punched it in several places, gave it to me, and handed me a two-shilling piece and two large copper pennies in change.

We drove a mile. Then we slowed to a stop, and I saw a uniformed man wearing a pistol emerge from a glassed-in shack and board the bus. My heart jumped. Mustafa had gotten out, he had called ahead, they were looking for me—

I looked at the man across the aisle from me. "Please," I said, "do you know why they've stopped us?"

"Customs check," he said. "It's just the garda seeing that no one's bringing something in from the free shopping center."

"They always do this?"

"They do."

I thanked him and tried to remain calm. Mustafa could not possibly have escaped yet, I told myself. He was probably still out cold. And even if he got loose, he would be a while figuring out how to burst stark naked upon the Irish scene without creating an uproar. And with no passport and no identification at all he might be in almost as much trouble as I was. So I ought to have a few hours' start, but still I wished I didn't have to look at any men in uniforms.

The garda climbed the stairs and walked the length of the aisle. Did anyone have anything to declare? No one did. He repeated the question in Gaelic, and still no one had anything to declare. He started toward the stairs again and then he stopped beside me, and I froze.

"American, are you?"

I managed a nod.

He touched my suit. "Fine cloth," he said, "but if

48

you'll permit me, sir, you might be finding it a bit thin for Ireland. Perhaps you'll buy yourself a good Irish jacket."

Somehow I smiled at him. "I'll do that," I said. "Thank you."

"Thank you, sir," he said and left, and the bus started up again. Some moments after that I began to breathe almost normally.

5

I left the bus in what I judged to be the center of Limerick City. The main business street was clean and neat and modest. It bustled with cars and cyclists, and I had difficulty crossing it. The traffice kept to the left, of course, and I kept wanting to look the wrong way as I stepped off the curb. An old woman on a bicycle very nearly ran me down.

The chill misty rain was still falling, and both the bus driver and the garda had noticed my suit and identified me at once as an American. I found a clothing shop and ducked inside. The clerk was tall and slender and young and black-haired, with the ascetic face of a seminarian. He was just about to close for the night. I bought a pair of gray woolen trousers and a bulky, tweed sport coat that must have weighed far more in pounds than the eight it cost. I added a black wool sweater and a checked cloth cap. The whole bill came to fourteen pounds and change, something like forty dollars.

"I have only American money," I said.

"Oh, I'm very sorry." he said.

"You can't accept it?"

"Oh, I can, but the banks are closed, sir. I'll have to charge you a sixpence on the pound for changing it."

I gave him a hundred dollars, and he computed everything very carefully with paper and pencil, then gave me my change in a mixture of English and Irish notes. He wrapped up my American suit very carefully with brown paper secured with heavy twine. He had thanked me when I made each of my selections and when I passed him the money. He thanked me once more when he gave me my change and again as he returned my wrapped suit. He grinned impishly as I stood with it under my arm.

"You look Irish now," he said.

"Do I?" I was pleased.

"You do. Good day, sir. And"—inevitably—"thank you."

I found a small dark pub on the side street. I was the only customer at the bar. A group of older men—all, I noted gladly, dressed in heavy sweaters and tweed sport coats and cloth caps—sat drinking Guinness and playing dominoes in a room off to the side. A woman poured me a stemmed glass of Irish whiskey and set a pitcher of water alongside it.

"Is it far to Croom?" I asked.

"Not far. Perhaps ten miles. Are you for Croom, sir?"

"I thought I might go there, yes."

"Have you a car?"

"No, I haven't. I thought I might take a bus. Is there a bus that goes to Croom?"

"There is, but I don't think there will be another tonight for Croom." She turned toward the domino game. "Sean? Is there a bus tonight for Croom?"

51

"Not until morning. It leaves at eight-thirty from the station near the Treaty Stone." To me he said, "It's to Croom you want to go, sir?"

"Yes."

"There's a bus in the morning, but none before. Could you wait until morning?"

By morning they would be combing Limerick for their escaped spy. "I hoped to go tonight," I said.

"It's not hard walking if you don't mind the rain. It would take you two hours, less than that if you're a good walker. Or you could rent a cycle for half a crown for the day. Mulready's will rent you one and give you good directions in the bargain. You'd be in Croom in less than an hour."

"Perhaps I'll do that."

"You're from America, are you?"

"Yes, I am."

"It's your first trip to Ireland?"

"Yes." And because a rushed visit to a hamlet seemed to require some explanation, I added, "I have an aunt in Croom. She was going to send someone to Limerick to pick me up in the morning, but I thought I'd go tonight to surprise her and save someone a trip."

"Did you want to start right away?"

"As soon as I can. I haven't been on a bike . . . a cycle in years. I'd rather not try an unfamiliar road in the dark."

"Mulready would see you got one with a good head-lamp. But you'd do well to start soon. If you'd care to walk with me"—he stood up from his domino game— "it's not far, and I'm headed that way myself, so I could take you to Mulready's shop."

It was, I was sure, very much out of his way; I had no doubt that he had planned to sit at his domino game for several more hours. But there seemed no way to refuse such graciousness. I managed to buy a round of drinks for the house, and then Sean insisted on buying one back. I was feeling the drinks as we walked through the rain down one street and over another, each narrower than the last. Sean wanted to talk about America. He had family in New York and Philadelphia and he thought John Kennedy might have saved the world had he lived a few years longer.

I gave my name as Michael Farrell and said I was from Boston. There were Farrells throughout County Limerick, he assured me, and surely many of them were my relatives.

John Mulready was in his bicycle shop, a dark and cluttered little establishment between a butcher shop and a tobacconist on a narrow street. Sean introduced me as a visitor from America come to stay with relatives in Croom, and could Mulready rent me a cycle for the trip? He could. And could he provide me with directions? He could, and with pleasure. I thanked Sean, and he thanked me, and we shook hands briskly, and he went back out into the rain.

Mulready was thick-bodied, florid-faced and fiftyish, with a brogue I had trouble understanding. He brought out a large cycle with a huge headlamp and an array of wires running here and there. He suggested I get up on it and see if it seemed the right size. I lifted myself gingerly onto the bicycle and wondered if I would be able to ride the thing. I told him I hadn't been on a cycle in years.

He was surprised. "Do they not have cycles in America, then?"

"Only for the children."

He shook his head in wonder. "Who would have thought it? The richest country in the universe, and only

53

the children may have cycles. Who would believe it possible?"

I asked him how much deposit he required. He didn't seem to understand, and I thought at first that he was having trouble catching the word, or that *deposit* was not the correct term in Ireland. It turned out that he recognized the word but not the concept. Why on earth would he care to take a deposit from me? Was I not a friend of Sean Flynn and would I not return the cycle when I had finished with it?

I asked the price. Two-and-six a day, he said, and less if I kept it a full week. I told him I'd need it for several days at least and reached for my money. He insisted that I pay him when I returned to save keeping records.

He told me the way to find the road to Croom and how to follow it. "You begin on the road to Adare and Rathkeale and Killarney, but you'll come first to Patrickswell and just past Patrickswell you'll turn south, and that will be on your left as you go. There will be a sign saying Croom so that you won't miss it. It's a good road, it is, paved all the way, and no more than ten or twelve miles from here to Croom."

I told him I had the directions down pat. He repeated them and insisted on drawing a rudimentary map for me to take along. I thanked him again, and he suggested that perhaps he might accompany me as far as the edge of the city so that I would get off on the right foot. I told him it was kind of him, but I was sure I would be all right. His expression suggested that he doubted this but was too polite to say so. He asked me how I liked Ireland. I said that I liked the country very much and that the people seemed to be the finest on earth. We shook hands warmly on that, and I wheeled my cycle out to the street and clambered onto it, hoping I wouldn't fall off at once and that he wouldn't see me if I did.

Cycling, I discovered, is like swimming; once learned, it is never wholly forgotten. The bike was unfamiliar and awkward for me. I seemed to be sitting too far off the ground and I had a bad time at first remembering that one braked by squeezing the metal gadgets on the handlebars. I kept trying to brake by reversing the direction of the pedals, which was how one accomplished the process when I was a boy—and how odd that I remembered it. And once I squeezed the handbrake accidentally, and the cycle stopped suddenly, and I did not. I flew from the cycle, the cap flew from my head, and a red Volkswagen had to swerve hard to the right to avoid demolishing the cycle and me.

But by the time I was out of Limerick City I had gotten the hang of it again. And then, with nothing to do but pedal the bike endlessly onward, with nothing to look at but green fields darkening in the twilight and occasional smooth stone huts with thatched roofs, with no greater hurdle than the occasional sheep and pigs that wandered about in the road and gazed into the cycle's headlamp, the whole hysterical madness of my situation came home to me. The reality of it had vanished in Limerick. The clothing store, the pub, the bicycle shop— each had provided conversation and warmth and motions to go through, words to say, a role to be played and lived with. There had been relatively little time to waste in thought.

Now, on an empty road to Croom, I had time to realize that my actions in the Shannon Airport men's room had been not those of James Bond but of a madman. I had escaped, but from what? A flight to my own country, a round of unpleasant but harmless questions put by the unpleasant but harmless agents of the Federal Bureau of Investigation, a possible loss of my passport (which action I could certainly appeal and probably overcome), and the impossibility of returning to Turkey for a shot at the cache of gold.

And now what had I accomplished? I had committed no crime to begin with and had very definitely committed one in escaping. I was like the innocent man who shoots the policeman who had been trying to arrest him by mistake. My original innocence had been entirely washed out. By now the U.S. Government would be very concerned about getting hold of me, and the Turks would be anxious to learn more of me, and the Irish police would be preparing to capture me. I could not go back to the States, I could not go back to Turkey, and I could not stay safely in Ireland. I was cold, I was starving, I was being rained upon, and I was getting cramps in my legs from pedaling the damned cycle up and down more damned hills than I had known existed.

Why should P. P. Dolan waste a minute on me? Why should he offend at least three governments by giving aid and comfort to a spy? And when I called myself a member of the Brotherhood, suppose he was a turncoat, an informer? I pictured Victor MacLaglen hulking in the doorway of a thatched hut. What would he do for me? Nothing. What *could* he do for me? Nothing.

I hit a stone and fell off the bicycle. By now, I thought, dragging myself to my feet and hauling the cycle to an upright position, by now I would be snug in the belly of a Pan American jet bound for Washington. In a few hours I would be explaining the foolishness of the situation to a pleasant young agent with a crew cut and a firm handshake. We would laugh together about the vagaries of the Turkish Government and the absurdity of our suspicion-ridden world. He would buy me a drink, I would buy him a drink, we would sit in a bar somewhere warm and dry, and in the morning, after a full evening of drunken camaraderie, I would take a train back to New York and my apartment and my books and my projects and my societies and my Kitty.

I mounted the bike and pressed onward.

I reached and passed the town of Patrickswell—a scattering of small shops, a church, a few dozen cottages. I seemed to have been riding forever. It was darker now, and the rain was coming down harder than before. I reached the fork in the road that pointed me toward Croom. I had been sure I would miss it, but I swung to the left and headed into a long downhill stretch that gave me a chance to stop pedaling, relax, and coast a while. I wished that I had stopped in Patrickswell for a drink and a bite to eat. I wished I had stayed in a pub in Limerick until it stopped raining, if it ever did stop raining in Ireland. I wished that the Irish Republican Brotherhood would do something about the damned rain. I wished I was on the plane for Washington.

Croom was small and silent, a nest of cottages, a two-story hotel, a block of storefronts in the center of town. I parked my cycle in front of a pub and went inside. It seemed to be a grocery store as well as a pub. There were two men at the bar drinking whiskey and another man behind the bar sipping beer. I had a drink of John Jameson. The three were talking in Gaelic.

In English I asked the bartender if he knew where P. P. Dolan lived.

He gave me tortuous directions. It seemed impossible that so small a town could hold a house so difficult to reach. I thanked him and went outside. The drink was making my head swim, and when I mounted the cycle again I didn't think I would be able to ride at all. The few minutes in the pub had been just enough time for my legs to knot up completely.

I followed the directions, made all the correct turns, and found the house. It was a small cottage, gray in the dim light. A television antenna perched on the thatched roof, and smoke trickled upward from the chimney.

I staggered to the door, hesitated, tried to catch my breath, failed, and rapped on the door. I heard footsteps, and the door was drawn open. I looked at the little man in the doorway and remembered the Victor MacLaglen I had visualized. This man was more a leprechaun, short, gnarled, with piercingly blue eyes.

"P. P. Dolan?"

"I am."

"Padraic Pearse Dolan?"

He seemed to straighten up. "Himself."

"You've got to help me," I said. The words flowed in a torrent. "I'm from America, from New York, I'm a member of the Brotherhood—the Irish Republican Brotherhood—and they're after me. I was in jail. I escaped when we reached Ireland. You have to hide me." And, gasping for breath, I dug out my passport and handed it to him.

He took it, opened it, looked at it, at me, at it again. "I don't understand," he said gently. "The picture's no likeness of you at all. And it says that your name is . . . let me see"—he squinted in the half light—"Mustafa Ibn Ali. Did I say that properly?"

6

"If you'll come inside and sit by the fire, Mr. Ali," the little man was saying. "It's cold outside, and so damp. And would you take a cup of tea, Mr. Ali? Nora, if you would be fixing Mr. Ali a cup of tea. Now, Mr. Ali—"

I had made two mistakes, it seemed. When I changed my summer suit for proper Irish clothing, I had transferred only one passport and the wrong one at that. My own passport remained in my suit. And my suit, so carefully wrapped by the young clerk, had somehow been separated from me. I had carried the parcel into the pub, but I hadn't had it with me when I left Mulready's cycle shop. I'd left it either at the pub or with Mulready, suit and passport and all.

"My name's not Mr. Ali," I said. "I took his passport by mistake. He's a Turk. He was my jailer in Turkey. He was taking me back to America when I escaped."

"You were a prisoner, then?"

"Yes." His face seemed troubled by this, so I added, "It was political, my imprisonment."

This eased his mind considerably. Nora, his daughter,

came over to us with the tea. She was a slender thing, small-boned, almost dainty, with milk-white skin and glossy black hair and clear blue eyes. "Your tea, Mr. Ali," she said.

"It's not his name after all," her father said. "And what would your name be, sir?"

"Evan Tanner."

"Tanner," he said. "Forgive me if I seem to pry, Mr. Tanner, but what led you to come here? To Croom and to my house?"

I told him a bit of it. He became quite excited at the thought that I was an American member of the Brotherhood and that I had heard of him. "Do they know of me, then, in America?" he mused. "And who would have guessed it?"

But it was Nora who seized on my name. "Evan Tanner. Evan Michael Tanner, is it?"

"Yes, that's right—"

"You know him, Nora?"

"If it's the same," she said. "And Mr. Tanner, is it you who writes articles in *United Irishmen?* Oh, you know him, Da. In last month's paper, the article suggesting that honorary representatives of the Six Counties be given seats in the Dail. 'Wanted: Representation for Our Northern Brethren,' by Evan Michael Tanner, and wasn't it the article you admired so much, and saying what a grand idea it was, and wouldn't you like to shake the hand of the man that wrote it?"

He looked wide-eyed at me. "And was it you who wrote that article, Mr. Tanner?"

"It was."

He took the tea from me. "Nora," he said, "spill this out. Bring the jar of Power's. And hurry over to Garrity's and fetch your brother Tom. I only wish my eldest son could be here, Mr. Tanner, for it's glad he'd be to meet you, a faithful member of the Brotherhood that he is, but the poor lad's in England now."

"Not in jail, I hope."

"No, praise God, but working in an office there. For what can a young man do to earn his keep in this god-forsaken country? Go quickly, Nora, and bring Tom back with you. And mind who you tell!" He shook his head sadly. "It's a hell of a thing to say," he explained, "but there are spies and informers everywhere."

The four of us, Dolan and Nora and Tom and I, listened to the latest developments in the Evan Tanner case on the kitchen radio. It seemed that Mustafa had seen a good number of James Bond movies, and they had served to supplement his account of my escape. According to the radio report, I was a dangerous spy of unknown allegiance being returned to America after attempting to infect all of Turkey with a plague of cholera. In the Shannon lavatory I had crushed a small pellet between my fingers, liberating a gas that temporarily paralyzed Mustafa's spinal column. Though he fought valiantly, he was in no condition to prevent my knocking him unconscious and trussing him up.

It was assumed that I had taken refuge in Limerick. The gardai were presently combing Limerick City, their numbers reinforced by a special detachment of plain-clothes detectives sent up from Dublin, and an arrest would no doubt be made in a matter of hours.

"It looks bad," I said. "Sooner or later they'll turn up the suit and spot the passport. Once they trace me to the bicycle shop, Mr. Mulready will be able to tell them that I went to Croom. And if they follow me this far, they'll be sure to find me."

"You're safe here," Dolan said.

"If the gardai come—"

"This house has been searched before," Dolan said. He drew himself up very straight. "Many times by the Tans and often enough by the Free State troops during the Civil War. Why, didn't my father hide half the Limerick Flying Column here? And when Michael Flaherty and the Dwyer boy did for that British lorry outside of Belfast, wasn't it here that they came? And hid in the upstairs room for three weeks before they got the boat for America. There's many a man on the run who's hid in Dolan's house, and never a one of them that's been taken. Nora will fix the attic room for you. You'll be comfortable enough in the bed, and the gardai could search this house ten times over and never set eyes on you."

"I couldn't let you take such a risk—"

"Don't talk nonsense. And don't be worrying about your suit, either. Most likely it's still unwrapped in Mulready's, waiting for you to come back for it. If you left it there, it's still there now. And if you left it in the pub, sure they'll take it to Mulready's, knowing you'll have to return to the cycle shop sooner or later. Tom can go for it tomorrow, and you'll have it in your hands without the gardai ever knowing of it."

"If they're already there and see him—"

"Tom will be looking for them, and if they're there, he will leave without being seen. Don't bother yourself about it, Mr. Tanner. But sit back, you must be tired. Are you after getting to bed right away or would you sit a while first?"

I said I would sooner sit and talk with him. Tom put a few more cakes of turf on the fire, and Nora freshened our drinks. She asked if I had been born in America, and I said I had, and she asked what part of Ireland my parents had lived in.

"Actually," I admitted, "I'm not Irish."

"In the Brotherhood and not an Irishman!"

My explanation filled them with wonder. Padraic Pearse Dolan got solemnly to his feet and stood gazing into the fire. "I've often said it," he said. "That men of goodwill throughout the world will rally to our cause, whether or not they be Irish. There are many demonstrations for the restoration of the Six Counties in America, are there not? The young people, the college students, with their marching and their picket signs?"

"But isn't that mostly for Vietnam?" Nora asked. "And civil rights and the hydrogen bomb?"

"Vietnam, civil rights, bombs, and Ireland—all one and the same," Dolan said. "It's that the whole world is Irish in spirit, wouldn't you say as much, Mr. Tanner?"

I agreed with this, and Nora filled our glasses again, and Tom took a harmonica from his pocket and began to play "The Boys From Wexford." He was short and slender, around nineteen or twenty, a few years younger than his sister and graced with the same dark good looks. We spent hours in front of the fire, finishing one jar of whiskey and tapping into a second, talking, singing, trading stories. Dolan had seen fighting, himself, on two occasions, against the Free State forces in 1932 and in the north a few years later. The earlier engagement had been the more heroic. He was only fifteen at the time and he lay in ambush with four lads not much older than himself. They trapped two Free State soldiers on a road near Ennis in County Clare and gunned them down. One was in the hospital for nearly a month, he said, and the other walks with a limp to this day. In the north they had lobbed six Mills bombs into a British post office. None had exploded, one of Dolan's group had two fingers of his left hand shot off, and the lot of them wound up spending six months in Dartmoor.

63

"Bloody British jail," he said. "What fine breakfasts they served us, though! You'd never get a breakfast like that in Ireland. Two slices of gammon and three eggs."

Nora sang "Danny Boy" in a high willowy voice that had us all crying, and I taught them a group of songs from the Rebellion of 1798 that not one of them had heard before. I told Dolan I'd learned them from a Folkways record and that they were traditional.

"Never heard a one of them," he said.

"They're folk music," I explained. "Handed down by the countryfolk from one generation to the next."

"Then that explains it," he said.

And midway through the second jar of whiskey I began talking about Turkey and why I had gone there. No one had asked; they had simply taken it for granted that I was a fine boy, that the Turks were heathens, and that any government with an unhealthy interest in me was surely in the wrong and thus merely illustrated the malevolence of officialdom. When I told of the fortune in Armenian gold their eyes went wide, and Nora sighed in amazement and shivered beside me.

"You'll have your fortune," Dolan pronounced. "You'll be wealthy, with acres of land and a house like a castle."

"I don't want the money for myself."

"Are you daft? You—"

I explained about the causes that had need of money. He seemed utterly astonished that I intended to endow, among several other worthy groups, the Irish Republican Army.

"You'll want to think that over," he said. "What would those bloody fools do with so much gold? They'd be after blowing up all of Belfast, and all be getting into trouble."

"They might regain the six counties," I said.

"Ah," he sighed, and his eyes took on a faraway look. "You're a fine boy, Evan. And it is a grand thing you would do."

I hadn't planned to talk about the gold, and if they had asked me I would probably have invented some convenient lie. But no one did ask, and so there was no reason to hide the truth. Besides, I almost had to talk about it now to make it at all real for myself. There in that cozy hut, with those fine warm people, there was no Turkey, no gold, no Mustafa, no toast and pilaff and pilaff. Only the rich singing of untrained off-key voices, and the warmth of roasting peat and peat-smoked whiskey, and the close sweet beauty of Nora.

When his father dozed off in front of the fire Tom Dolan showed me to my room. It was reached through a trapdoor in the second-floor ceiling. Tom stood on a chair, moved a lever, and a flap dropped from the ceiling, releasing a rope ladder. I followed Tom up the ladder and into a long, narrow room. The ceiling, less than four feet high in the center, sloped to meet the floor on either side. A mattress in the center of the room was piled generously high with quilts and blankets. Tom lit a candle at the side of it and said he hoped I wasn't the sort who grew nervous in cramped quarters.

"To shut up tight," he said, "you haul in the ladder and then catch hold of that ring in the panel with the stick. Draw it shut and fasten it, you see, and it cannot be opened from below. And no one would think there's a room up here, with so little space and no window. Will you be all right here?"

"It seems comfortable."

"Oh, it is. I'd be here myself, and you in my bed,

but Da wouldn't allow it. He says you must be secure if the gardai come." He hesitated. "How is it in America, Mr. Tanner?"

"Evan."

"Do they pay good wages there? And are jobs to be had? My brother Jamie's been after me to come to London, but what I've heard of America—"

"Don't you want to stay in Ireland?"

"She's the finest country in the world, and the finest people in it. But a man ought to see something of the world. And there's not such an abundance of things to occupy a younger man in Croom. Unless one's a priest or a drunkard. I'm nineteen now, and I'll be out of here before I'm twenty-one, God willing."

He clambered back down the rope ladder and tossed it up to me, then raised the panel so that I could catch it with the hooked stick. I locked myself in, blew out the candle, and stretched out on my mattress in the darkness. It was still raining, and I could hear the rain on the thatched roof.

I was tired, and my body ached from the cycling. I went through the Hatha Yoga relaxation ritual, relaxing groups of muscles in turn by tightening them and letting them relax all the way. When this was completed I did my deep, measured, breathing exercises. I concentrated on an open white circle on a field of black, picturing this symbol in my mind and thinking of nothing else. After about half an hour I let myself breathe normally, yawned, stretched, and got up from the mattress.

I went downstairs. The turf fire still burned in the hearth. I sat in front of it and let myself think of the gold in Balikesir. My mind was clearer now, and I felt a good deal better physically, with the effects of the whiskey almost completely worn off.

It's difficult to remember what sleep was like or how

I used to feel upon awakening; sensory memory is surprisingly short-lived. I do not believe, though, that sleep (in the days when I slept) ever left me as refreshed as twenty minutes or an hour of relaxation does now.

The gold. Obviously I had gone about things the wrong way. It would now be necessary to approach the whole situation through the back door, so to speak. I would stay in Ireland just long enough for the manhunt for the notorious Evan Michael Tanner to cool down a bit. Then I would leave Ireland and work my way through continental Europe and slip into Turkey over the Bulgarian border. I would set up way stations along the route, men I could trust as I had trusted P. P. Dolan.

Europe was filled with such men. Little men with special schemes and secret dark hungers. And I knew these men. Without asking an eternity of questions, without demanding that I produce a host of documents, they would do what they had to do, slipping me across borders and through cities, easing me into Turkey and out again.

Was it fantastic? Of course. Was it more fantastic than lying on a mattress between the ceiling and the thatched roof of an Irish cottage? No, not really.

I was, I thought, rather like a runaway slave bound for Canada, following the drinking gourd north, stopping at the way stations of the Underground Railway. It could be managed, I realized. It needed planning, but it could be managed.

I was so lost in planning that I barely heard her footsteps on the stairs. I turned to her. She was wearing a white flannel wrapper and had white slippers upon her tiny feet.

"I knew you were down here," she said. "Is it difficult for you to sleep up there?"

67

"I wasn't tired. I hope I didn't wake you?"

"I could not sleep myself. No, you were quiet, I didn't hear you, but I thought that you were down here. Shall I build the fire up?"

"Not on my account."

"Will you have tea? Oh, and are you hungry? Of course you are. What you must think of us, pouring jars of punch into you and giving you nothing to eat. Let me fry you a chop."

"Oh, don't bother."

"It's no bother." She made a fresh pot of tea and fried a pair of lean lamp chops and a batch of potatoes. We ate in front of the fire and afterward sat with fresh cups of tea. She asked me what I was going to do. I told her some of the ideas that had been going through my mind, ways of getting back into Turkey.

"You'll really go, then."

"Yes."

"It must be grand to be able to go places, just to go and do things. I was going to take the bus to Dublin last spring, but I never did. It's just stay home and cook for Da and Tom and care for the house. It's only a few hours to Dublin by bus. Can you ever go back to your own country, Evan?"

"I don't know," I said slowly.

"For if you're in trouble there—"

"I hadn't even thought of that. I can't go back now, but when it all blows over—"

"You could stay in Ireland, though." Her eyes were very serious. "I know you're after getting the gold now, but when you've taken the treasure and escaped with it, why, if you couldn't get back to America, you could always come to Ireland."

"I don't think the Irish Government cares too much for me just now."

"Sure, you're a ten-day wonder, but they'll forget you. And anyone can get into Ireland. It's getting out of Ireland that everyone's after, you know. You could come back."

I realized, suddenly, that she had put on perfume. She had not been wearing any scent earlier in the evening. It was a very innocent sort of perfume, the type a mother might buy her daughter when she wore her first brassiere.

"Are you a Catholic, Evan?"

"No."

"A Protestant, then."

"No. I don't have a religion exactly."

"Then, if you wanted to, you could become a Catholic?"

"If I wanted to."

"Ah."

"I thought of it once. A very good friend of mine, a priest, made a fairly heroic effort to convert me. It didn't take."

"But that's not to say it couldn't some other time, is it?"

"Well, I don't think—"

She put her hand on mine. "You *could* come back to Ireland," she said slowly, earnestly. "Not saying that you will or won't, but you *could*. And you *could* turn Catholic, though not saying will or won't." Her cheeks were pink now, her eyes bluer than ever in the firelight. "It's a sin all the same, but not so serious, you know. And if Father Daly hears my confession, instead of Father O'Neill, he won't be so hard on me. Ah, Nora, hear yourself! Talking of the confession and penance before the sin itself, and isn't that a sin of another sort!"

We kissed. She sighed gratefully and set her head on my chest. I ran a hand through her black hair. She raised her head and our eyes met.

69

"Tell me lies, Evan."

"Perhaps I'll come back to Ireland, and to Croom."

"Ahhh!"

"And perhaps, God willing, I'll find my faith."

"You're the sweetest liar. Now one more lie. Who do you love?"

"I love you, Nora."

We crawled through the trapdoor to my little crow's nest between ceiling and roof. I retrieved the ladder and the panel and closed us in. No one would hear us, she assured me. Her father and brother slept like the dead, and sounds did not carry well in the cottage.

She would not let me light the candle. She took off her robe in a corner of the room, then crept to my side and joined me under all the quilts and blankets. We told each other lies of love and made them come true in the darkness.

There had, I found, been other liars before me, a discovery that filled me at once with sorrow and relief.

Afterward she slept, but only for a few moments. I held her in my arms and drew the covers over us both. When she awoke she touched my face, and we kissed.

"A tiny sin," she said, not very seriously this time.

"Hardly a sin at all."

"And if I'd been born to be perfect, they'd surely have put me away in a convent, and then who would care for Da?"

She left me, found her robe, opened the trapdoor, and started down the ladder. "Now," she said, "now you'll sleep."

70

7

- -

In the hours before breakfast I read a popular biography of Robert Emmet and several chapters from *The Lives of the Saints*. Around five-thirty I stepped outside the cottage. A mist was rising from the countryside and melting under the glow of false dawn. The air had a damp chill to it. It was not raining, but it felt as though it might start again at any moment.

A few minutes past six Nora came down and started breakfast. She wore a skirt and sweater and looked quite radiant. Her father and brother followed a few minutes later. We ate sausages and eggs and toast and drank strong tea.

Before long I was alone again. Tom had gone to return the bicycle and retrieve my suit and passport, Nora was off for church and then a round of shopping, and Dolan had left to join a crew mending a road south of the town. I sat down with a pad of notepaper and a handful of envelopes and began writing a group of cryptic letters. It would be well, I felt, to leave as soon as possible and it would probably not be a bad idea if some of my prospective hosts on the continent had a vague idea that they were about to have a clandestine house guest on their hands. I couldn't be sure what route I might take, what borders would be hard to cross or where I would be unwelcome, so I wrote more letters than I felt I could possibly need. The intended recipients ranged as far geographically as Spain and Latvia, as far politically as a Portuguese anarcho-syndicalist and a brother and sister in Roumania who hoped to restore the monarchy. I didn't expect to see a quarter of them, but one never knew.

I made the letters as carefully vague as I could. Some of my prospective hosts lived in countries where international mail was opened as a matter of course, and others in more open nations lived the sort of lives that made their governments inclined to deny them the customary rights of privacy. The usual form of my letters ran rather like this:

> *Dear Cousin Peder,*
> *It is my task to tell you that my niece Kristin is celebrating the birth of her first child, a boy. While I must travel many miles to the christening, I have the courage to hope for a warm welcome and shelter for the night.*
> *Faithfully,*
> *Anton*

The names and phrasing were changed, of course, to fit the nationality of the recipient and the language of each letter was the language of the person to whom it was sent. I finished the last one, sealed them all, and addressed as many envelopes as I could. I couldn't remember all the addresses but knew I could learn most of the ones I was missing in London. Almost all my groups have contacts in London.

I couldn't mail the letters from Croom, of course, and wasn't sure whether or not it would be safe to mail them all from the same city, anyway. But at least they were written.

When Nora came back to the cottage she kept blushing and turning from me. "I'm to have nothing to do with you," she said.

"All right, then."

"Must you accept it so readily?"

I laughed and reached for her. She danced away, blue eyes flashing merrily, and I lunged again and fell over my own feet. She hurried over to see if I was all right, and I caught her and drew her down and kissed her. She said I was a rascal and threw her arms around me. We broke apart suddenly when there was a noise outside, and the door flew suddenly open. It was Tom. His cycle— or mine, or Mr. Mulready's—was in a heap at the door-step.

"Mr. Tanner fell down," Nora began, "and I was seeing whether he'd broken any bones, and—"

Tom only had time for one quick doubting look at her. He was out of breath, and his face was streaked with perspiration. "The old woman at the pub found your suit," he said. "Went to the gardai. They traced you to Mulready, and the fool said you were bound for Croom, and there's a car of them on the road from Limerick. I passed them coming back."

"You passed them?"

"I did. They had a flat tire and called for me to help them change it. Help them! Two of them there were,

73

and having trouble changing a tire. I asked where they were headed for, and they said Croom, and I said I'd be right back and give them a hand, and I came straight here. They'll be here soon, Evan. They'll ask at the tavern and find out you went there for directions to our house. You'd best go to your room."

"I'll leave the house."

"And go where? In Limerick City they say that more are coming over from Dublin, and detectives from Cork as well. Go to your room and stay quiet. They'll be on us in five minutes, but if you're in your room they'll never find you."

I grabbed up my letters and snatched up the sweater I had been wearing. I opened the panel, scurried up the rope ladder, and drew it up after me. Tom raised the panel and locked it from below.

Perhaps it was only five minutes that I crouched in the darkness by the side of the trapdoor. It seemed far longer. I heard the car drive up and then the knocking at the door. I caught snatches of conversation as the two policemen searched the little cottage. Then they were on the stairs, and I could hear the conversation more clearly. Nora was insisting that they were hiding no one, no one at all.

"You bloody I.R.A.," one of the police said. "Don't you know the war's over?"

"It's not yet begun," Tom said recklessly.

The other garda was tapping at the ceiling. "I stayed in a house just like this one," he was saying. "Oh, it was years ago, when I was on the run myself. Stayed in half the houses in County Limerick and a third in County Clare. What's the name here? Dolan?"

"It is."

"Why, this is one I stayed in," the garda said. "A hiding place in the ceiling, if I remember it. What's this?

Do you hear how hollow it sounds? He's up there, I swear it."

"And that's your gratitude," Nora said. "That Dolan's house saved your life once—and may we be forgiven for it—only so that you can betray the house, yourself."

The garda was evidently working the catch to the panel. I had secured the hook on the inside, and although he opened it, the panel would not drop loose.

"That was years ago," I heard him say.

"Gratitude has a short memory, does it?"

"Years and years ago. And why keep old hatreds alive?" He'd loosened the panel slightly, enough so that his fingers could almost get a purchase on it. He tugged at it, and I felt the hook straining. It was old wood. I didn't know if it would hold.

"We're a republic now," the other garda said. "Free and independent."

"A free and independent republic under the bloody heel of the bloody English Parliament." This last from Tom.

"Oh, say it at a meeting. At a parade."

The garda had a better grip on the panel now. The hook-and-eye attachment couldn't take the strain. It was starting to pull loose.

"You're wasting your time," Nora said desperately.

"Oh, are we?"

"He was here, I'll not deny it, but he left this morning."

"And contrived to fasten the hook up there after himself, did he? I hope you don't expect an honest Irish policeman to be taken in by a snare like that, child."

"And did I ever meet one?"

"Meet what?"

"An honest Irish policeman—"

At that unfortunate moment the hook pulled out from the wood, and the panel swung open all the way, the garda following it and falling to the floor with the sudden momentum. The other reached upward, caught hold of an end of the rope ladder and pulled it free. I was in darkness at the side of the opening. I could see down, but they apparently did not see me.

The policeman who had forced the panel was getting unsteadily to his feet. The other turned to him and drew a revolver from his holster. "Wait here," he said. "I'll go in there after him."

"Take care, Liam. He's a cool one."

"No worry."

I thought suddenly of the men's toilet at Shannon Airport. I watched, silent, frozen, as the garda climbed purposefully up the rope ladder. He used one hand to steady himself and held the gun in the other. His eyes evidently didn't accustom themselves to the dark very quickly, for he looked straight at me without seeing me. A Vitamin A deficiency, perhaps.

I glanced downward. The other garda stood at the bottom of the ladder, gazing upward blindly. Tom was on his left, Nora a few feet away on the right, her jaw slack and her hands clutched together in despair. I glanced again at the climbing garda. He had reached the top now. He straightened up in the low-ceilinged room, and he roared as his head struck the beam overhead.

I took him by the shoulders and shoved. He bounced across the room, and I threw myself through the opening in the floor, like a paratrooper leaping from a plane. Between my feet, as I fell, I saw the upraised uncomprehending face of the other garda.

"Up the Republic!" someone was shouting. It was days later when I realized that it was my voice I had heard.

8

It was neither as easy nor as glorious as the assault upon Mustafa, but it had its points. The garda dodged to one side at the last possible moment. Otherwise my feet would have landed on his shoulders, and he would have fallen like a felled steer. Instead, I hit him going away, caromed into the side of him, and he and I went sprawling in opposite directions. I scrambled to my feet and rushed at him. He was clawing at his revolver, but he had buttoned the holster and couldn't open it. He had white hair and child-blue eyes. I swung at him and missed. He lunged toward me, and Tom kicked him in the stomach just as Nora brought her shoe down on the base of his skull. That did it; he went down and out.

I barely remembered the trapdoor in time. I rushed to it, threw the rope ladder upward and saw the end of it strike the upstairs garda hard enough to put him off stride. I swung the panel back into place. He got his balance and lunged for it, and his fingers got in the way. He roared as the panel snapped on them. I opened it, and he drew out his fingers, howling like a gelded camel, and I closed the panel again and held it while Tom fastened the catch in place.

"It won't hold him," Nora said.

"I know."

"If he jumps on it—"

"I know."

But he wasn't jumping on it. Not yet. The prostrate policeman was starting to stir, and the one in the attic room was kicking at the panel. Sooner or later he would leap on it with both feet and come through on top of us. I raced down the stairs and out the door. Their car, a gray Vauxhall sedan with a siren mounted on the front fender, was in front of the cottage. They had left the keys in the ignition, reasoning, perhaps, that no one would be such a damned fool as to steal a police car.

I wrenched open the door, hopped behind where the wheel should have been. It was the wrong side, of course. I got behind the wheel and turned the ignition key, and the car coughed and stalled. I tried again, and the motor caught. I fumbled for the hand brake, released it, shifted into first, and pulled away from the curb.

There's no spare tire, I thought idiotically. They had that damned flat, so there's no spare tire, and this is dangerous—

It was definitely dangerous. I heard a gunshot and saw the white-haired cop firing at me from the second-floor window. Evidently he had recovered. Evidently he had remembered how to unbutton his holster and get at his gun. And the other one had jumped through the trapdoor after all, because he was coming out the doorway toward me.

I put the accelerator pedal on the floor and went away.

• • •

The car was even worse than the bicycle had been. It had been months since I'd driven any sort of car, and I'd never driven one with right-hand drive. The Vauxhall kept drifting over to the wrong side of the road, moving into the lane of oncoming traffic as if with a will of its own. The road curved incessantly, and I continually found myself coming around a curve to encounter a Volkswagen or Triumph approaching me on the right, at which point I automatically pulled to the right and charged the little car, making for it like a bull for a muleta. I generally swung back to the left in time, but once I forced a VW off the road and no doubt scared the driver half to death.

To make matters worse, I had no particular idea where I was going until a road sign indicated I was headed for a town called Rath Luirc. I had never heard of it and didn't know whether it lay north, south, east, or west of Croom. When I reached the town and passed through it I found that the same road went on to Mallow and ultimately to Cork. This was better than returning to Limerick, but it wouldn't get me to Dublin, or to London, or to Balikesir. I was driving a stolen police car in hazardous fashion with no real destination in mind, and somehow this struck me as a distinctly imperfect way to proceed.

A few miles past Mallow I took a dirt road to the right, drove for a mile or so, and pulled off to the side of the road. The dirt road saved me the need of keeping the car on the left side, as the entire road was only a car's width wide. If I'd met anyone headed in the opposite direction, things might have become difficult, but this didn't happen. The road looked as though it didn't get much use.

I got out of the car. A trio of black-faced sheep, their sides daubed with blue paint, wandered over to the heaped-stone fence and regarded me with interest. I walked around the car and got back inside. There was a road map of Ireland in the glove compartment. I opened it and found out approximately where I was. I was approximately lost.

I put the map aside and sorted through the remaining treasures in the glove box. Three sweepstakes tickets, a flashlight, a 4*d*. postage stamp with the head of Daniel O'Connell, a small chrome-plated flask of whiskey, a pair of handcuffs sans key, a St. Christopher medal on a gold-plated chain, and half of a ham sandwich neatly wrapped in wax paper. I ate the sandwich, drank a bit of the whiskey, put the flashlight in one pocket and the flask in the other, and fastened the St. Christopher medal around my neck; I was one traveler who would need all the help he could get.

The rest I left in the car. I would have liked to take the handcuffs, feeling that I might be likely to have a use for them sooner or later, but they could not be used without a key. I checked the Vauxhall's trunk before I left and found only a flat tire, a bumper jack, a tire iron, and a lug wrench. I could not foresee a use for any of these and left them all behind. I rolled down the windows and left the key in the ignition, a procedure which, in New York, would have guaranteed the imminent disappearance of the car. But I couldn't be sure this would happen in rural Ireland. One could not count on turning up juvenile delinquents on unpaved one-lane roads. At the least, I could hope that no one took the road for a few hours so that the car would remain undiscovered that long.

I walked back to the main road. My side road had also been headed toward Cork, with a branch cutting off toward Killarney and points west. Thus, whoever found the car might conclude that I was headed in that direction, had car trouble, and continued toward either Cork or

Killarney on foot. I didn't know how well this would throw them off the trail or for how long, but it was something. For my part, I started walking toward Mallow. I'd gone less than a mile when a car stopped, and a youngish priest gave me a lift the rest of the way.

All he wanted to talk about was the American spy. He hadn't heard about my escape in Croom, but he'd heard a strong rumor that I was in Dublin plotting to dynamite de Valera's mansion. I passed myself off as a Scot from Edinburgh spending a few months learning the Gaelic tongue in County Mayo and now touring the Irish countryside. He wasn't sufficiently interested in me to pursue the matter far enough to find the holes in my story.

I mailed about half of my letters in Mallow. A copy of the Cork *Examiner* had my picture on the front page. I pulled my cap farther down on my forehead and hurried to the bus station. There was a bus leaving for Dublin in a little over an hour, the ticket clerk told me. I had enough Irish money for a ticket and bought one. There was a darkened pub across the street. I had a plate of fried whiting and chips and drank a glass of Guinness and kept my face in the paper until it was time to catch my bus. Boarding it, presenting my ticket, walking all the way through the bus to the very back, I felt as conspicuous as if I had no clothes on. No one seemed to notice me. I'd bought a batch of paperbacks at the bus station and I read them one after another, keeping my face hidden as much as possible all the way.

We stopped for dinner in Kilkenny, then went on to Dublin through Carlow and Kildare and Naas. By sunset it had begun raining again. It was almost nine o'clock when the bus reached the terminal in Dublin. The whole trip was only 150 miles or so, but we'd had many stops and several waits. I left the bus and found the terminal crawling with gardai. Several of them looked right at me without recognizing me.

In the men's room I had a drink of whiskey from the flask, then capped it and put it back in my jacket pocket. My pockets were bulging with the flask and the flashlight. I slipped out of the terminal through a rear exit. I walked in the rain through a maze of narrow streets, not sure where I was or where I ought to be going. When I came to O'Connell Street, the main street of downtown Dublin, I felt as though I must be going in the right direction. And then I remembered that hunted men always headed for the largest cities and sought out the downtown sections of those cities with all the instinct for self-preservation of moths seeking a flame—the police always looked for hunted men in the busy downtown sections of big cities.

A pair of James Bond movies were playing in a theater a few doors down from the remains of the Nelson monument. The I.R.A. had dynamited the top of the monument a few months earlier, and the city had blown up the rest of it but hadn't yet put anything in its place. A tall man with glasses and a black attaché case was looking at the monument, then glanced at me, then looked at the monument again. I went into the cinema and sat in the back row for two and a half hours, hoping that Sean Connery could give me some sort of clue as to what I might do next. I had a pocketful of American money that I didn't dare spend, a handful of English and Irish pounds, a flashlight, a flask of whiskey (which I emptied and discarded in the course of the second film), and a St. Christopher medal. I did not have a passport, or a way of getting out of Ireland, or the slightest notion of what to do next.

James Bond was no help. Near the end of the second

picture, just as Bond was heaving the girl into the pot of molten lead, I saw a man walking slowly and purposefully up and down the aisle, as if looking for an empty seat. But the theater was half empty. I looked at him again and saw that he was the same man who had looked alternately at the Nelson monument and at me. There was something familiar about him. I had the feeling I'd seen him before at the bus station.

I sank down into my seat and lowered my head. He made another grand tour of the cinema, walking to the front and back again, his eyes passing over me with no flicker of recognition. I couldn't breathe. I waited for him to see me, and then he walked on and out of the theater while I struggled for breath and wiped cold perspiration from my forehead.

But he was there when I came out. I knew he would be.

I tried to melt into the shadows and slip away to the left, and at first I thought I had lost him. When I looked over my shoulder, he was still there. I walked very slowly to the corner, turned it, and took off at a dead run. I ran straight for two blocks while people stared at me as if I had gone mad, then turned another corner and slowed down again. A cab came by. I hailed it, and it stopped for me.

"Just drive," I said.

"Where, sir?"

I couldn't think of the answer to that. "A pub," I managed to say. "Someplace where I can get a good dinner."

The cab still had not moved. "There's a fine restaurant just across the street, sir. And quite reasonable, as well."

My man came around the corner. He didn't have his attaché case now, I noticed. I tried to hide myself, but he saw me.

I said, "I had a row with my wife. I think she's following me. Drive around the block a few times and then drop me off at that restaurant, can you?"

He could and did. My pursuer had stepped to the curb now and was trying to hail a cab of his own. My driver charged forward as the light turned. I watched out of the back window. The man had still not caught a cab. My driver turned a corner, drove for a few blocks, then turned another corner. I settled back in the seat and relaxed.

I kept checking the back window. Now and then I saw a cab behind us and had the driver turn corners until we lost it. Finally he told me no one could possibly have followed us. "I'll take you to that restaurant now, sir. You'll have a good meal there."

He dropped me in front of the restaurant. As I opened the door I glanced over my shoulder and saw the tall man with glasses. He was still trying to catch a cab. He saw me, and our eyes met, and I felt dizzy. I pushed open the door of the restaurant and went inside. When I looked back, I saw him crossing the street after me.

The headwaiter showed me to a table. I ordered a brandy and sat facing the door. I had never before felt so utterly stupid. I had escaped and then, brainlessly, I had returned to precisely the place where the tall man was waiting.

The door opened. The tall man came in, looked my way, then glanced out the door again. His face clouded for a moment and he seemed to hesitate. Perhaps, I thought, he was afraid to attempt to capture me by himself. No doubt I was presumed armed and dangerous.

Could I make a break for it? Surprise had worked twice before, with Mustafa and the two gardai. But I couldn't avoid the feeling that the third time might be the charm. This man was prepared. He was walking toward my table—

Still, it seemed worth a try. I looked past him as though I did not see him, my hands gripping the table from below. When he was close enough I would heave it at him, then run.

Then over his shoulder I saw the gardai—three of them, in uniform—coming through the doorway. If I got past him, I would only succeed in running into their arms. It was as though I were drowning. All at once my official misdeeds of the past two days rushed through my mind: assaulting a Turk, entering Ireland illegally, traveling with false papers, bicycle theft, assault and battery of two Irish policemen, auto theft, auto abandonment, resisting arrest—

The tall man with the glasses stumbled, fell forward toward me. His right hand broke his fall, his left brushed against my right side. He said, "Mooney's, Talbot Street," then got to his feet and swept past me.

And the gardai, solemn as priests, walked on by my table and surrounded him. One took his right arm, the other his left, and the third marched behind with a drawn pistol. They marched him out of the restaurant and left me there alone.

I could only stare after them, I and all the other patrons of the restaurant. It was late, and most of the other diners were about half-lit. At the doorway the tall man made his move. He kicked backward at the garda with the pistol, wrenched himself free from the grasp of the other two, and broke into a run.

Along with other diners, I pressed forward. I heard two short blasts on a police whistle, then a brace of gunshots. I reached the door and saw the tall man rushing across the street. A garda was shooting at him. The tall man spun around, gun in hand, and began firing wildly. A bullet shattered the restaurant window, and I dropped to the floor. A fresh fusillade of shots rang out. I peered over the window ledge and saw the tall man lying in a heap in the middle of the street. There were sirens wailing in the distance. One of the gardai had taken a bullet through one hand and was bleeding fiercely.

And no one was paying any attention to me.

I went back to my table. My hands were trembling. I couldn't control them. I thought for a moment that I must have gone schizophrenic, that it was I who attempted to escape the police and who was shot down by them, and that it was a symptom of my madness that I thought it had happened to someone else. The waiter brought my brandy. I drank it straight down and ordered another.

Mooney's, Talbot Street, he had said. I didn't know what he meant, or who he was, or who he thought me to be. Why had he followed me? If the police were following him, why should he follow me? What was Mooney's? Was I supposed to meet him there? It seemed unlikely that he would ever keep the appointment.

Then I found in my right coat pocket, where he must have placed it when he fell, a metal brass-colored disc perhaps an inch and a half across. Stamped upon it were the numerals 249.

At that point it was easy enough to figure out the what, if not the why. I worked my way back to O'Connell Street and found Talbot Street, just around the corner from the cinema. Mooney's was a crowded pub halfway down the block. I found the checkroom and presented the brass disc. As I had expected, the attendant handed over the black attaché case, and I left a shilling on the saucer. I closed myself in a cubicle in the men's room and propped the attaché case upon my lap. It was not locked. I opened it.

On top was an envelope with my name on it. I drew

a single sheet of hotel stationery from it. The message was in pencil, written in a hurried scrawl:

> Tanner—
> I just hope you're who I think you are. Deliver the goods to the right people and they'll take care of you. The passports are clean. Big trouble for everybody if delivery isn't made.

Six hours later I was in Madrid.

9

Esteban Robles lived on Calle de la Sangre—Blood
Street—a dim, narrow two-block lane in the student
quarter south of the university. The morning was hot,
the sun blindingly bright, the sky a perfect cloudless blue.
I abandoned my heavy jacket at the airport and changed
some British pounds for pesetas at the Iberian Airways
desk.

My cab driver had some difficulty finding Calle de la
Sangre. He tore furiously up and down the narrow streets
of the quarter and chatted about the weather and the bulls
and Vietnam. My Spanish was South American, and I
told him I was from Venezuela. We then discussed the
menace of Fidel. He wanted to know if it was true that
the Fidelistas gelded priests and ravished nuns. The
thought infused him with scandalized lust.

I found Robles on the third floor of a drab tenement
permeated with cooking smells. His room resembled the
cell of a slovenly monk—a desk piled high with books
and newspaper clippings and cigarette stubs, another heap

of books in a corner, four empty wine bottles, a pan of leftover beans and rice, and a narrow cot that sagged in the middle. The floor was incompletely covered with linoleum, its pattern obscured by years of dirt. Robles himself was a young fellow with the body of a matador and the bearded face of a protest marcher. I knew him as a fellow member of the Federation of Iberian Anarchists. It was a dangerous thing to be in Spain, and I had trouble convincing him that I was not an agent of the Civil Gaurd.

Perhaps I shouldn't have bothered. If he had gone on thinking of me as an agent of Franco's secret police, he would have cooperated with me. Instead, I went to great lengths to convince him who I was and I only succeeded in terrifying him. He kept darting stricken looks at the door of his room, as if men with drawn sabers might burst in at any moment and lead us both off to prison.

"But what do you want here?" he kept demanding. "But why do you come to me?"

"I have to go to Turkey," I explained.

"Am I an airplane? This is not safe. You must go."

"I need your help."

"My help?" He glanced again at the door. "I cannot help you. The police are everywhere. And I have nowhere for you to stay. Nowhere. One small bed is all I own, and I sleep in it myself. You cannot stay here."

"I want to get out of Spain."

"So do I. So does everyone. I could make a grand fortune in America. I could become a hairdresser. Jackie Kennedy."

"Pardon me?"

"I would set her hair and make a fortune."

"I don't think I—"

"Instead, I rot in Madrid." He fingered his beard. "I could set Jackie Kennedy's hair and make a fortune. Lady

Bird Johnson. Are you a hairdresser?"

"No."

"I have had no breakfast. There is a café downstairs, but you cannot go. They will shoot you in the street like a dog. Can you speak Spanish?"

We had been speaking Spanish all along. I was beginning to suspect that Robles was mad.

"There is a café," he said. "They know me there. So they will not give me credit." He glanced at the door again. His fear was so genuine that I was beginning to share it. At any moment the Civil Guard would come in and shoot us down like hairdressers.

"I have no money," he said.

I gave him some Spanish money and told him to get breakfast for both of us. He snatched the notes from me, glanced again at the door, lit a cigarette, smoked furiously, dropped ashes on the floor, then threw himself on the cot.

"If I order breakfast for two," he said, "they will know I have someone up here."

"Tell them you have a girl."

"Here? In this goat pen?"

"Well—"

"They know me," he said sorrowfully. "They know I never have a girl. You should never have come here. Why did you leave America? Mamie Eisenhower. Who sets her hair?"

"I don't know."

"You create trouble. How can we eat? No one will believe you are a girl. Your hair is too short."

I suggested that he eat breakfast at the café and buy food for me. He leaped from the bed and threw his arms around me. "You are a genius," he shouted. "You will save us all."

When he went out, I tried to lock the door. The lock

was broken. I sat on his bed and read a poor Spanish translation of Kropotkin's essay on "Mutual Aid." He had evidently read it over many times as the text was extensively underlined, but the underlining made no sense at all. He underlined trivia—unimportant adjectives, place names, that sort of thing.

He came back with some sweet rolls and a cardboard container of *café con leche*. While I ate he told me of his breakfast—four eggs, slices of fried ham, fresh juice, a dish of saffron rice with peas and peppers. I listened to all this while I ate my rolls and sipped the bad coffee.

"I will get another bed," he said. "Or, if that is not possible, you may sleep upon the floor. My house is your house."

"I won't be staying that long."

"But you must stay! It is not safe in the streets. They would shoot you like a dog." He smiled engagingly. "You will stay," he said, "as long as you have money."

"Oh."

"Have you much money?"

"Very little."

He looked at the door again. "On the other hand," he said, "you would perhaps be uncomfortable upon the floor. And it is not safe here. Every day the police come and beat me. Do you believe me?"

"Yes."

"You do? You should have stayed in America. What do you want from me?"

"A few hours of solitude. I want the use of your room for several hours and then I want you to take me to someone who can help me get out of Spain."

"You will go to Portugal?"

"No. To France."

"Ah. Now you want me to leave?"

"Yes."

"Why?"

"I want to sleep."

"In my bed?"

"Yes."

"It is not sanitary."

I took some more Spanish money from my wallet. "You could pass a few hours in the cinema," I suggested.

He was gone like a shot. I closed the door and wished that it had a functioning lock on it. I went to the window and drew the shade. It was badly torn. Through the hole in the shade I looked into a room in the building next door. A rather plump girl with long black hair was dressing. I watched her for a few moments, then left the window and sat on Esteban's bed and opened my black attaché case. A gift of Providence, I thought. An ideal survival kit for a hunted man. It had everything I might need—money, passports, and documents so secret I had no idea what they were.

Along with the unsigned and unintelligible note, the attaché case had contained a heavy cardigan sweater with a London label, a change of underwear, a pair of dreadful Argyle socks, a safety razor with no blades, a toothbrush, a can of tooth powder made in Liverpool, and a Japanese rayon tie with a fake Countess Mara crest. There was also a Manila envelope holding banded packages of British, American, and Swiss currency—two hundred pounds, one hundred fifty dollars, and just over two thousand Swiss francs. Another larger envelope contained three passports. The American passport was in the name of William Alan Traynor, the British in the name of R. Kenneth Leyden, and the Swiss for Henri Boehm. Each showed a rather poor photograph of the tall man.

On the American passport he was wearing glasses. On the other two he was not.

A third Manila envelope, carefully sealed with heavy tape, held the mysterious documents. These, evidently, were the "goods" that I was to deliver to "the right people." I had attempted to slit the tape with my thumbnail in the manner of James Bond opening a packet of cigarettes. This proved impossible, so I had laboriously peeled off the tape in the privacy of the Dublin lavatory and had a look at the contents of the parcel. It had made no particular sense to me then; now, in the equally dismal atmosphere of Esteban Robles' dirty little room, it remained as impenetrable as ever.

Half a dozen sheets of photocopied blueprints. Blueprints for what? I had no idea. A dozen sheets of ruled notebook paper covered with either the mental doodling of a mathematician or some esoteric code. A batch of carefully drawn diagrams. A whole packet of confidential information, no doubt stolen from someone and destined for someone else. But stolen from whom? And destined for whom? And indicating what?

When I first opened the case it had scarcely mattered. I had packed everything away and taken a taxi to the Dublin airport. There were no flights to the Continent until morning, I learned, unless I wanted to fly first to London and then make connections to Paris. I did not want to go to London at all, not now. I used the American passport to buy a ticket to Madrid and paid for it with American money. I left the case in a locker and went back into town. At the lost and found counter of the bus station I explained that I'd left a pair of glasses on a bus, and asked whether anyone had turned them in. Five pairs were brought to me, and I would have liked to try them on until I found a pair that wasn't too hard on my eyes, but this might have aroused suspicion. I picked a pair that looked rather like the ones in William Alan Traynor's passport photograph and thanked the clerk and left.

By flight time I was back at the airport. I took my attaché case from the locker, lodged the envelope of unidentifiable secret papers between my shirt and my skin, and incorporated the currency with my own small fund of money. I tucked my two extra passports (and Mustafa Ibn Ali's) into a pocket, combed my hair to conform to the passport photo, and put on the glasses. Their previous owner had evidently combined extreme myopia with severe astigmatism. I hadn't worn them five minutes before I had a blinding headache.

I'd have preferred using another passport and going without glasses, but there were good reasons for being Traynor. The glasses did change my appearance somewhat, and with my own photo plastered over every newspaper in Ireland it seemed worthwhile to avoid being recognized as Evan Michael Tanner. Besides that, the Traynor passport was the only one with an Irish entry visa stamped on it. The tall man had evidently used it to enter Ireland six weeks earlier.

I got blindly through customs, with my attaché case receiving only a cursory check. The flight to Madrid was happily uneventful, the landing smooth enough. The Aer Lingus stewardess made cheerful announcements in English and Irish and served reasonably good coffee. I kept my glasses on and kept my eyes closed behind them. Whenever I looked at anything, it blurred before my eyes, and my head ached all over again.

Once I was through Spanish customs, I dug out the R. Kenneth Leyden passport and showed it as identification when I changed pounds to pesetas at the Iberia desk. I put the glasses away, hoping I would never have to wear them again, and headed for the one man in

Madrid who could help me on my way to Balikesir.

At the time, never having met Esteban Robles, I had had no idea he was a lunatic.

The packet of secret papers bothered me. If I had known just what they were, I might have had some idea what to do with them. Knowing neither their source nor their destination nor their nature, I was wholly in the dark.

I could destroy them, of course, but that might prove to be a bad idea if they were as valuable as they seemed to be. I could mail them anonymously to the Irish Government—the Irish certainly seemed anxious to recover them. I could send them to the American Consulate, thereby doing what could only be regarded as patriotic while passing the buck neatly enough.

And yet, in a sense, I felt a sort of debt to my anonymous benefactor, the tall man who had been shot down by the Irish police. However invalid his assumptions of my identity, however suspect his motives, he had done me a good turn. He had provided me with three passports to spirit me out of Ireland and away from the manhunt that sooner or later would have caught up with me. He had endowed me with a supply of capital that would help me on my way to Balikesir. My own funds were perilously close to being depleted, and his pounds and dollars and francs were welcome.

He had also supplied me with a change of underclothing and socks, which I now put on. It is difficult, if not impossible, to wear the socks and underwear of a dead man without feeling somehow obliged to carry out his mission. But who was he? And which side was he on?

He was not on the Irish side; that much was obvious. All right, then, suppose he was an enemy of Ireland.

Why would he be spying on Ireland? What precious information could the Irish possibly have that he or his employers would want? And who could his employers be? The British? The Russians? The CIA? The answer was unattainable without a knowledge of the nature of the documents, and they remained as impenetrable as ever.

At least no one knew I had them. I could destroy them or retain them or send them somewhere and, for better or for worse, I would be forever out of it. Unless—

It was a horrible thought.

It was possible, I thought suddenly, that the tall man had let someone know what he'd done with the documents. He could have sent off a wire or dashed off a fast letter to his employers. *They're on to me but I'm sending the stuff with your man Tanner,* he might have wired.

And someone at the other end would have realized that Tanner was not their man at all, and that he ought to be gotten hold of in a hurry. And then what?

Things, I thought, were getting awfully damned involved.

I looked at my three passports. If the tall man had spread the word, those passports were dangerous. His men would probably know the names he was using— Traynor and Leyden and Boehm. If he was a Yugoslavian spy, for example, it would not do to present any of the three passports at the Yugoslavian border. But this left me as much in the dark as ever. If I only knew for whom he worked, I could avoid those countries. But I didn't. Maybe he was a *Spanish* spy, as far as that went—though why Spain would be spying on Ireland I could not imagine.

I was getting nowhere. I gave it up, put everything back in the attaché case, closed it, and stretched out on Esteban's unsanitary bed. My head was spinning, my stomach recoiling from the combined effect of fear and bad coffee. I went through my little repertoire of Yoga exercises, relaxing, breathing deeply, and generally easing myself out of my blue funk.

Esteban had still not returned when I got up from the bed. I tucked my attaché case under the bed and left the room. In a bookstore near the university I bought a pocket atlas and calculated a route to the French border. I stopped at a café and had a glass of bitter red wine. I thumbed through the atlas again and plotted the remainder of my trip. Spain, France, Italy, Yugoslavia, and Turkey—that seemed the best route. That gave me four borders to cross, with each one promising to be slightly more hazardous than the one before it. But it could be done. I was certain it could be done.

Esteban was waiting for me. He ran to me and embraced me furiously. "You were gone," he said accusingly. "When I came back, you were gone."

"I went out for some air."

"Ah, who can breathe in the fetid stench of fascism? But the streets are dangerous. You should not have gone out. I feared that something might have happened to you."

"Nothing did."

"Ah." He scratched at his beard. "It is not safe for you here. It is not safe for either of us. We must leave."

"We?"

"Both of us!" He spread his arms wide as if to embrace the beauty of the idea. "We will go to France. This afternoon we rush to the border. Tonight, under the cloak of darkness, we slip across the border like sardines. Who will see us?"

"Who?"

"No one!" He clapped his hands. "I know the way, my friend. One goes to the border, one talks to the right people, and like that"—he snapped his fingers soundlessly—"it is arranged. In no time at all we are across the border and into France. I will go to Paris. Can you imagine me in Paris? I shall become the most famous hairdresser in all of Paris."

"Are you a hairdresser in Madrid?"

He frowned at me. "One cannot be a hairdresser in Madrid. Would Jackie Kennedy come to Madrid to have her hair set? Or Christine Keeler? Or Nina Khrushchev? Or—"

"Have you ever been to France?"

"Never!"

"Have you been to the border?"

"Never in my life!"

"But you know people there?"

"Not a soul!" He could not contain himself and rushed to embrace me again. His body odor was almost identical to that of Mustafa.

"I don't know," I said. "I'm not sure it sounds like the best of all possible plans. It might be dangerous for us to travel together."

"Dangerous? It would be dangerous for us to separate."

"Why?"

"Why?" He spread his hands. "Why not?"

"Esteban—"

He turned from me and walked to the window. "She is not there now," he said. "There is a girl across the way, very fat. Sometimes one can see her."

"I know."

"Sometimes she has a man there, and I watch them together. Not always the same man, either. I was going to watch her tonight. It is sad, is it not? Tonight I will be in France and I will never be able to watch the fat girl again. Do you think she is a whore?"

"No. Maybe. I don't know. What does it—"

"Perhaps she would come to France with us. I will set her hair and she will become famous."

I reached under the bed for my attaché case. I wanted only to escape this madman. The case was not there.

"Esteban—"

"You look for this?" He handed it to me. I opened it and checked its contents. Everything seemed to be there.

"You see," he said solemnly, "it would be very dangerous for us to be separated. Every day at four o'clock the Guardia Civil comes to check on me. They do not beat me—that was something I made up for you—but they come every day to make sure I am still here. I am subversive."

"I believe it."

"But they do not feel that I am dangerous. Do you understand? They only check to see who it is whom I have been seeing and what correspondence I have received and matters of that sort. I always tell them everything. That is the only way to deal with these fascist swine. One must tell them everything, everything. Only then can they be sure that I'm not dangerous."

If they thought the foul little lunatic was not dangerous, then they did not know him as well as I did.

"So if they come today, I must tell them about you. The names on your three passports, and the papers with the letters and numbers upon them, and—"

"No."

"But what else can I do, my friend? You see why we must go to France together? If we are separated, the police will know all about you. But if we are together, then you are safe. And under the protective cloak of darkness we will steal across the border into France, and

I will become famous. We are like brothers, you and I. Closer than brothers. Like twins who shared the same womb. Do you comprehend?"

I was taller than Esteban, and heavier. I thought of knocking him down and fleeing, but I had done that too often lately. It couldn't work forever. Sooner or later one would run out of beginner's luck. And, if there was any truth in that old chestnut about a madman's possessing superhuman strength, Esteban would be able to wipe the floor with me.

"When will the Guard visit you?"

"In a few hours. So you see that it is good you came to me. In all of Madrid it was to Esteban Robles that you came. Is it not fate?"

In all of Madrid, it was to Esteban Robles that I came. Of all my little band of conspirators, of all my troupe of subversives and schemers and plotters, I had sought out the Judas goat of the secret police. And now I had to take the madman with me to France.

"If you want to go to France, why don't you just go?"

"I have no money, my brother."

"If I gave you money—"

"And I am not clever. I am an artist, a grand artist, but I am not clever. Do I know anything about crossing borders? About stealing through the pass under the protective cloak of night? I know nothing. But with you to guide me and to bribe the proper persons—"

"I could give you money."

"But we *need* each other, my friend!"

Perhaps, I told myself, he might prove useful. At least he spoke Spanish like a native, a natural enough accomplishment for a Spaniard, but one that might be of use. No, I decided, he would *not* prove useful. He would be a nuisance and a danger, but I had to take him along. I was stuck with the lunatic.

"We will go?"

"Yes," I said.

"Now?"

"Now."

He went to the window. "She is still not in her room. Shall we wait for her? The fat little whore would probably be happy to accompany us to Paris."

"No."

"No?"

"No."

"You do not like fat girls? For my part—"

"We go together," I said. "Just the two of us, Esteban. You and I. No one else."

His eyes were unutterably sad. "I never have a girl," he said. "Never, never, never. The one time I found a girl who would go with me, I was fooled. You know how I mean? I thought it was this pretty American girl, but when we got back to my room, it turned out to be a *marica* from New York. A fairy. It was better than nothing, but when one has one's heart set on a girl—you are sure you do not want the fat little—"

"There will be girls in Paris, Esteban."

"Ah! You are my brother. You are more than my brother. You are—"

Words failed him, and I was again suffocated in his embrace.

10

Before we went anywhere, I took Esteban to a barber and had him shaved. He fought the idea every step of the way, but I managed to convince him that Frenchmen did not wear beards. Without it he looked less like a fiery anarchist and more like a backward child. I had the barber give him a haircut while he was at it and had my own hair cut so that it looked a little more like the passport photos and a little less like the picture of Evan Tanner that the newspapers had printed. Then, with Esteban in one hand and the attaché case in another, I left Madrid.

We took a train as far as Zaragoza, a bus east to Lérida and another bus north to Sort, a small village a little over twenty miles from the frontier. In Zaragoza I left Esteban for a few moments at a restaurant while I visited a few shops and spent a few pesetas. He was still eating when I returned. He slept on the bus ride. The bus to Sort was not heated, and the last lap of our journey was cold, with the sun down and the wind blowing through the drafty bus. I gave the tall man's sweater to Esteban, who promptly went back to sleep. I wished that I had kept my Irish jacket or had brought along a flask of brandy.

At Sort I poked Esteban awake and led him off the bus. He lit a cigarette and blew smoke in my face. He had been doing this all the way from Madrid, and it was beginning to annoy me.

"Are we in France?"

"No."

"Where are we?"

"Some place called Sort."

"In Spain?"

"Yes."

"I have never heard of it."

There were four cafés in the town. We visited each of them and drank brandy. The third of the four turned out to be the worst, so we returned to it. Esteban appeared to be about half-lit. Among his many other talents, he was evidently incapable of holding liquor.

We sat in a dingy back booth. He began talking in a loud voice about the joys of Paris and the need to escape from the reeking stench of fascism. I had two choices— I could try to sober him up or I could get him drunk enough to pass out. I had the waitress bring a full bottle of brandy and I poured one shot after another into Esteban, and ultimately his head rolled and his eyes closed and he sagged in his chair and quietly passed out.

I stood up and walked to the bar. A large man with sad eyes and a drooping moustache stood beside me. "Your friend," he said, "says things which one should not say in the presence of strangers."

"My friend is sick," I said.

"Ah."

"My friend has a sickness in his mind and must go for treatment. He must go to the hospital."

"There is no hospital in Sort."

"We cannot stay in Sort, then, for I must take him to a hospital."

"There is a hospital in Barcelona. A fine modern hospital, where your friend would be most comfortable."

"We cannot go to the hospital in Barcelona. There is only one hospital that will care for my friend properly."

"In Madrid, then?"

"In Paris."

"In Paris," he said. I poured us each a brandy. He thanked me and said that I was a gentleman, and I said that it was pleasant to drink in the company of worldly men like himself.

"It is far," he said slowly, "to Paris."

"It is."

"And one must have the right papers to cross the frontier."

"My friend has no papers."

"He will have difficulty."

"It is true," I said. "He will have great difficulty."

"It will be impossible for him."

"For worldly men," I said carefully, "for worldly men of goodwill, men who understand one another and understand how life is to be lived, I have heard it said that nothing is impossible."

"There is truth in what you say."

"It is as I have heard it said by wiser men than I."

"It is a wise man who listens to and remembers the words of other wise men."

"You do me much honor, señor."

"You honor me to drink with me, señor."

We had another brandy each. He motioned me to follow him, and we sat at the table next to Esteban. He was still asleep.

"Call me Manuel," the man said. "And I shall call you what?"

"Enrique."

"It is my pleasure to know you, Enrique."

"The pleasure is my pleasure."

"Perhaps among my acquaintances there are men who could help you and your unfortunate friend. When one lives in a town for all of one's life, one knows a great many people."

"I would greatly appreciate your help."

"You will wait here?"

"I will," I said.

He stopped at the bar and said something to the bartender. Then he disappeared into the night. I ordered a cup of black coffee and poured a little brandy into it. When Esteban opened his eyes, I made him drink more of the brandy. He passed out again.

Manuel returned while I was still sipping my coffee. Two other men accompanied him. They stood in the bar and talked in a language I did not understand. I believe it was Basque. The Basque language is one I do not speak or understand, an almost impossible language to learn if one is not born to it. The grammatical construction is as much of a nightmare as the language of the Hopi Indians. I felt very much at a disadvantage. I am not used to being unable to understand other people's speech.

Manuel left his companions at the bar and approached our table. "I have consulted with my friends," he said. "They are of the opinion that something can be done for you."

"May God reward their kindness."

"It must be this night."

"We are ready."

He looked doubtfully at Esteban. "And is he ready, also?"

"Yes."

"Then come with me."

I had trouble getting Esteban to his feet. He swayed groggily and offered up dramatic curses to fascism and the state of the beautician's profession in Madrid. Manuel turned to his friends at the bar, touched his head with his forefinger, then pointed at Esteban and shrugged expressively. He took one of Esteban's arms, and I took the other, and we walked him out into the night.

The other two men followed us. Half a mile from the café we entered a dingy one-room hut. The smaller of Manuel's two friends, with long sideburns and denim pants frayed at the cuffs, moved around the room lighting candles. The other uncapped a flask of sweet wine and passed it around. I didn't let Esteban have any. It seemed time to sober him up a bit.

Manuel introduced us all around. The small man with the sideburns was called Pablo; the other, fat, balding, and sweaty, was Vicente. I was Enrique and Esteban was Esteban.

"I have it that you wish to go to France," Vicente said.

"Yes, and to Paris."

"I will set the hair of Brigitte Bardot," said Esteban.

"But the border is difficult."

"So I have heard."

Pablo said something quickly in Basque. Vicente answered him, then turned to me and resumed in Spanish. "You and your friend have a sympathetic reason for going to France. You must take your friend to a hospital, is it not so?"

"It is so."

"For such fine purposes, one can bend laws. But you must know, my friend, that these are dangerous times. Many smugglers attempt to take contraband over the border."

106

I said nothing. Manuel said something in Basque. I was furious that I had never been able to learn the language. I remembered one sentence that I had stubbornly committed to memory. *"I will meet you at the jai alai fronton."* The Basque construction for this is torture— *I the jai alai fronton at which is played the game of jai alai in the act of meeting I have you in the future.* I don't know how the Basques learn it.

"So you see," said Vicente, "that it is necessary for us to examine your possessions so that we may assure ourselves that you are not smugglers."

"I see."

"For we help willingly but only when the motives of those we help cannot be called into question."

I propped the black attaché case on a rickety card table and opened it. Pablo and Vicente gathered around, while Manuel stayed with Esteban. The various papers were passed over without a second glance. The clothes attracted no particular attention. The items I had purchased in Zaragoza received the lion's share of attention.

"Ah," said Vicente. "And what is this?"

"Beautician supplies."

Esteban came rushing over to me. "For my salon!" He embraced me. "You are my friend, my brother. What have you bought for me?"

"Your supplies, Esteban."

"My brother!"

Pablo was sorting through the bag of cheap cosmetics I had picked up. There were several plastic combs, a pair of scissors, some hair curlers, hardly the elaborate equipment one would use in a beauty parlor. He picked up a tin box of face powder, opened it, sniffed, and looked at me with raised eyebrows.

"Face powder," I said.

Vicente licked a finger, dipped it into the can of face

powder, licked it again, smiled, and said something in Basque to Manuel and Pablo. They began to laugh happily.

"Perhaps you will leave this here," Vicente said.

"But it is necessary that we take it with us."

"Ah, but can you not get better face powder in Paris? The French are renowned for their cosmetics, so I have heard."

"This is special powder."

"I can see that it is."

"We have a great need for it."

"A face powder with little scent to it," Vicente said. "A face powder with a sweet taste, and yet a bitter undertaste. This is a most remarkable powder."

"My friend obtains great results with this powder."

The three of them laughed uproariously. Esteban was utterly baffled. He couldn't understand what was so important about a tin of powder or what caused men to laugh over it. I did not enlighten him.

Vicente dropped the tin of powder back into my attaché case. I closed the case, and Vicente threw a heavy arm around my shoulder. "We can help you," he said. "And I think you are wise to take the face powder with you, for it would be difficult to locate this brand in Paris, would it not?"

"Most difficult."

"For so many powders are applied with a powder puff, and this one requires a needle, does it not?"

I said nothing.

"We will take you to the border, Enrique. But we must go now."

"That is good."

"And I will carry your suitcase."

I looked at him.

"In case you are searched, señor. It is advisable."

108

"But in the suitcase—"

"The face powder, my friend."

We played with that one. Finally he agreed that he would carry the powder only at the moment of crossing. Pablo asked to see the tin again. I opened the case and showed it to him. He left hurriedly, explaining that he had to obtain provisions for the journey. Vicente brought out the flask of wine, and we drank to the success of our travels.

When Pablo returned, we got under way. Manuel said good-bye to us and headed back to the café. Vicente led us to a donkey cart piled high with straw. Elaborately, he explained to me how the crossing would be managed. He needn't have bothered. I had seen the scene in countless films. At the border, he told me, we would ride on the wagon with the straw covering us, while he and Pablo rode in front. Thus, he said, delighted with his own ingenuity, the border guards would think there was only a load of straw on the wagon, when actually there would be two men beneath the straw whom they would not see.

"Two men and an attaché case," I said.

"Of course," Vicente said. He looked terribly sad. "Now the arrangements of the money," he said. "We have expenses, you understand. Certain money must be passed on to certain persons. I am sure you comprehend—"

"How much?"

He quoted a price that came to less than $50 U.S. I had a feeling he would spend that much or more bribing the border guards. I started to bargain, just to avoid being too delighted with the price, and he almost instantly knocked it down a third. He wanted this fare, I realized. He wasn't about to let us walk away.

I paid him the money. It would be a long ride, he said, and no doubt we would wish to sleep. We could stretch out on top of the hay and cover ourselves with blankets and we need not get under the hay until he told us. It would be easiest to cross the frontier at the corner of Andorra, he said. We would cross two borders, first passing from Spain into Andorra, then from that tiny Basque republic into France. But that, he said, was much the easiest way. The guards were less vigorous at those posts, and they were his friends.

Esteban and I climbed onto the hay. Pablo gave us each a blanket, and we stretched out on the hay and wrapped ourselves in the blankets. The night was cooler now, the sky alive with stars. Pablo and Vicente climbed up on the little platform behind the donkey, and the animal shifted into gear and started for the border. I lay still, watching the stars, my hand coiled tightly around the grip of the attaché case.

In the darkness Esteban whispered, "But your name is not Enrique."

I told him to be still. Then, after I thought he had dropped off to sleep again, he was back with more questions. "When did you buy me those supplies? The equipment for the beauty parlor?"

"I will tell you later."

"Tell me now."'

I looked over at our two escorts. I wondered if they could hear or if it would matter.

I said, "I bought them for you in Zaragoza."

"It was good of you."

"Don't mention it."

"But if I may say so, my brother, I think you were cheated."

"How?"

"The shears are cheap. They won't last. And the cosmetics are of the poorest sort. On a shop girl one might use such inferior goods, but on the wife of Charles de Gaulle—"

"You'll set her hair?"

"And make a fortune. What is all this fuss about the face powder?"

"It is forbidden to bring face powder into France."

"But why?"

"There is a very high tariff. To protect the French manufacturers, you see."

"But to make such a fuss over one tin? And I heard the fat one say that it has no smell and tastes sweet."

"Go to sleep, Esteban."

"There are many things that I do not understand."

"Do you want to go to Paris?"

"With all my heart, friend."

"Then go to sleep."

He fell silent. His was a hurt silence at first. He wanted me to hold his hand and tell him how good it would be for him in Paris, how they would welcome him to the town, how he would set the hair of the world's most important women. He was a madman and a nuisance, yet in his own disquieting way he was good company for a trip of this sort. He gave me an unusual amount of self-confidence. He was so utterly lost, so incapable of coping with any situation, that by comparison I felt myself wholly in command of things.

The donkey moved steadily onward. Smoke from Vicente's cigar wafted back over us. The road we followed wound slowly uphill, leveling off now and then, circling in and out of the mountains, then climbing upward at a sharper inclination. I lay with my eyes closed and did my Yoga exercises from time to time, getting as much rest as I could. It was at times like this, times when one had to spend several hours doing nothing at all, that

111

I envied those who slept. Esteban could close his eyes and lose touch with the world. He could blank out his mind to all but dreams and pass over several hours in an instant of subjective time. I had to lie there in the dark with nothing to do but wait.

This had not bothered me in years. Once I originally adjusted to going without sleep, I had always contrived to have something to do, someone to talk to, something to read or study. No matter how long one lives, awake or asleep, one can never know all that there is to know. There are, for example, several hundred languages spoken throughout the world. It would take the greater portion of a lifetime to learn them all. Alone in my apartment, stretched out on my bed listening to a stack of learn-while-you-sleep records, I could rest mind and body and add another language to my collection—and not grow bored.

Lying on a mound of hay, staring at the stars and listening to the sounds of the night and the snores of Esteban and the occasional incomprehensible chatter of Vicente and Pablo, was as bad in its own way as rotting for nine days in an Istanbul jail cell.

I thought of getting up, getting out of the wagon and running alongside the donkey for a while. Or perhaps I could sit with Pablo and Vicente and talk with them in Spanish. The donkey seemed to be moving at about six or seven miles an hour. We were twenty miles from the frontier, and with the circuitous route we were following it seemed likely that we would travel forty miles to go twenty. It would be dawn or very close to it before we reached the border, and I did not feel like lying in the straw for that long a time.

As it turned out, it was a good thing I stayed where I was.

112

• • •

I heard Pablo speaking Spanish. "I believe we may stop now. They have not moved or made a sound for some miles."

"You are certain?"

"Call to them. See if they answer."

Vicente called out, "Enrique? Are you asleep?"

I did not say anything. I heard Esteban shift in his sleep and wanted to hit him with something. He had to remain still now, or we were in trouble.

"They are sleeping, Vicente."

"All right."

The cart slowed, then stopped. I heard them drop down from the driver's platform and come around to the rear of the cart.

"They sleep."

"Can you be sure?"

A hand touched my foot, raised it a few inches, then let it fall. I stayed limp.

"They sleep, Vicente. It is time to take the powder. Later will be difficult."

"But he said that he would let me carry it across the border for him."

"He will think of something by then. Some trick."

"You are right. Perhaps—"

"No."

"In one instant I could slash both their throats. I would draw two red lines upon their necks, and they would be no cause for worry. And then—"

I tensed in the darkness. I saw him in my mind, knife drawn, bending over us. I could kick out, I thought. Kick out hard and then jump backward and hope to throw myself clear. I could—

"And when their friends come? Surely you do not think that ones like this could carry something of such importance themselves. Their clothes are poor, and their shoes worn. The powder is worth a fortune."

"They are couriers, then."

"Couriers, yes. And if they do not arrive, there will be trouble, and men will come looking for them. But if they arrive without the powder, they will be in trouble themselves."

"I do not know, Pablo—"

Keep talking, Pablo. I thought. Keep talking.

"It is all the more reason why we will make the switch now," Pablo went on. "Then later we will ask to carry the powder across the border. This Enrique will argue with us. We will finally let him have his own way. Then, when he discovers the powder is gone, he will know that someone else must have taken it. That it was not we who did it."

"Where is it?"

"In the case he carries."

"Ah."

Hands fastened on the attaché case and took it gently from my loose grasp. The catch was opened. A few seconds later hands slid the case back where it had been, fastened once more.

"He will never know," said Pablo.

"And the other?"

"Nor will the other?"

"The other is a madman."

"I think not," said Pablo. "I think they are very clever, these two, and that the other only pretends to be a madman. One may do well at times by pretending to be that which one is not." The sentence sounded involved enough to be a word-for-word translation from the Basque. "I think the madman is the brains of the pair."

114

"But the other does all the talking and carries the powder—"

"Of course," said Pablo. "As I said, they are clever."

I made a great show of waking up half an hour later, yawning, stretching, having a moment's trouble orienting myself, then swinging down from the hay cart and walking alongside the donkey. I wondered how close Vicente had come to drawing a red line on my throat.

"When we cross into Andorra," Pablo said, "you will want us to carry the powder for you."

"Perhaps."

"Ah, it is necessary."

"Perhaps. If we are under the straw, we will be safe, will we not?"

"One would hope so."

"Then why should not the powder be safe with us?"

His explanation was involved and, I think, purposely unconvincing. If we were discovered, he said, he could bribe a guard to overlook the fact. But if the powder were found, there would be trouble, and so it would be better to let him take it. It would, he assured me, be quite safe in his hands.

"Are we close to the border?"

"Very close. An hour, perhaps two."

I went back to the wagon. When we approached the Andorran border, Pablo stopped the cart again and made us burrow ourselves underneath the hay. He asked for the powder.

"If they search you," I said, "and find the powder, you will be in great difficulty. But if they search us and find it, you can deny that you knew what we carried and thus save yourself from trouble."

He let me outfumble him for the check. He and

Vicente piled hay on us, and we lay there under the smelly hay while the wagon started up again. Esteban was still half asleep and very much confused. At first he tried to fight his way free of the hay. I finally managed to calm him down, but he obviously didn't like it.

"I do not trust those men," he said. "Do you?"

"Of course not."

"No? I think they are thieves and entirely ruthless. I think they would kill us without a second thought."

"I agree."

"You do?"

"Vicente was going to kill you while you slept. But Pablo would not let him."

"He was going to kill me?"

"With a knife," I said. "He was going to slit your throat."

"Mother of God—"

"But it's all right now," I assured him.

And it was. The border was easily crossed. Pablo and Vicente evidently did quite a bit of smuggling and were well known at that station. The wagon passed through without incident, continued on through the postage stamp republic of Andorra, and cleared French Customs on the other side. I felt a little sad about this. I was one of the few Americans actually to travel to Andorra and I saw nothing whatsoever of it, spending my entire passage through the country at the bottom of a load of hay. When one could neither see anything nor understand the language, I thought, one might as well have stayed home and watched it all on television.

I was a little worried about ditching Pablo and Vicente, but it turned out that they were more anxious to get away from us than we were to see the last of them. We had a ceremonial drink of wine together, and they went their way, and we went ours, walking north into France. In the first café we came to we ordered breakfast, and I opened the attaché case and drew out the little tin of face powder.

"I do not understand," said Esteban.

"I bought this in Zaragoza," I explained. "I bought a tin of face powder and spilled it out and replaced the powder with confectioner's sugar and crushed aspirin. It was supposed to taste like heroin, and I guess it passed the test. You see, they would hardly have smuggled us across the border out of charity. There had to be profit in it for them, and a tin of heroin would represent a fairly elaborate profit."

He was nodding eagerly.

"Do you remember when Pablo left the hut in Sort to obtain supplies? He ran off to buy a can of face powder. Then while you slept they switched cans with us. So we started with face powder and now we wind up with face powder." I gave the can to Esteban. "For you," I said. "For your salon in Paris."

"Then we never had any heroin?"

"Of course not."

"Oh. And they do not have heroin now, do they?"

"They have a dime's worth of sugar and a nickel's worth of crushed aspirin. That's all."

"Ah."

"If they sniff it," I said, "they're in for a big disappointment."

11

It was almost impossible to explain to Esteban that we were not going to Paris together. He insisted that brothers such as we could not be separated and he ultimately began to weep and tear at his hair. I did not want to go to Paris. There was a man I had to see in Grenoble, near the Italian border. I tried to put Esteban on a Paris train, but he would have no part of it. I had to come with him, he insisted. Without me he would be lost.

The irritating thing was that I knew he was telling the truth. Without me he definitely would be lost, and I couldn't help feeling an annoying sense of responsibility for him. For a time I toyed with the thought of taking him with me. This, though, was plainly out of the question. He had been enough of a liability in his native land. In Italy, in Yugoslavia, in Turkey, he would be a fatal burden.

When I had recovered the gold, when I had dispatched the mysterious documents to the proper place, when I had somehow cleared myself with the Irish police and the Turkish police and the American authorities and whatever other national bureaus had developed an interest in me, then I could find some way to take care of Esteban. In the meanwhile he would survive. He was too mad to get into serious trouble.

And so we boarded a train to Paris, Esteban and I. We got on the train at Foix, and I got off it at Toulouse and took another train east to Nîmes and a bus northeast to Grenoble. M. Gerard Monet must have already received the cryptic note I'd sent him from Ireland. I went to his home. His wife said that he was at his wine shop— it was not quite noon—and told me how to find him. I walked to the shop and introduced myself as Pierre, who had written from Ireland. He put a finger to his lips, walked past me to the door, closed it, locked and bolted it, drew a window shade, and took me behind the counter.

He was a dusty man in a dusty shop, his hair long and uncombed, his eyes a brilliant blue. "You have come," he said. "Tell me only what I must do. That is all."

"My name is—"

He held up one hand, corded with dark blue veins. "But no, do not tell me. A man can repeat only what he knows, and I wish to know nothing. My father was of the movement. My great-grandfather fell at Waterloo. Did you know that?"

"No."

"For all my life I have been of the movement. I have watched. I have listened. Will anything come of it? In my lifetime? Or ever? I do not know. I will be honest with you, I doubt that anything will come of it. But who is to say? They tell me the days of Empire are over for all time. The glory of France, eh? But I do what there is for me to do. Whatever is requested, Gerard Monet will perform what he is capable of performing. But tell me nothing of yourself or your mission. When I drink,

119

I talk. When I talk, I tell too much. What I do not know I can tell no one, drunk or sober. You understand?"

"Yes."

"What do you require?"

"Entry to Italy."

"You have papers?"

"Perhaps."

"Pardon?"

"I don't know whether or not they're valid. I'd rather slip across the border, if that can be arranged."

"It can. It can, and with ease."

He picked up the telephone, put through a call, talked rapidly in a low voice, then turned to me. "You can leave in an hour?"

"Yes."

"In an hour my nephew will come to drive you to the border. There are places where one may cross. First we shall lunch together."

"You are kind."

"I know how to serve. The Monets have always known how to serve. Do you go to Corsica? No, do not tell me. I have never been to Corsica. Let us have lunch."

We had rolls and cheese and some rather good wine. Afterward Monet poured cognac for each of us. We raised our glasses to toast the eternal memory of Napoleon Bonaparte and pray for a speedy restoration of his line to power in France. I made my brandy last. He had three more before his nephew arrived.

"A grand occupation for such as me," he said, waving a hand to include the shop. "Eh? A wine shop for a drunkard, a dusty shop for a man with impossible dreams. You will not tell them that I drink?"

"No."

"You are a good man. I drink up all the profits. I talk when I drink. Tell me nothing."

"All right."

The nephew was my age, dark, sullen, handsome, and uncommunicative. He drove a Citroën. The car was silent, the ride soft, the countryside beautiful under a hot sun. The nephew did not ask me who I was or why I wanted to go to Italy. He did not seem to care.

"The old man is crazy," he said once.

I did not answer.

"He thinks he's Napoleon."

"Oh?"

"Crazy," he said. And that was all he said for the rest of the ride. He stopped the car finally at the side of the road—a narrow road winding through hilly country. From here, he said, I would have to walk cross-country. He pointed the way through the fields and asked me if I had something with me to cut the wires. I did not. He grumbled, rummaged through the trunk of the Citroën, and found a pair of wire-cutting pliers.

"I don't suppose you'll be able to return these," he said. "They're not cheap, you know. Every time the old bastard calls me, it costs me money. He must think I'm made of it."

I offered to pay him for the pliers. He said they cost twenty-five francs, a little over five dollars. This was obviously untrue, but I paid the money, and he left without a word.

I walked about a mile through the countryside to the six-foot barbed-wire fence dividing France and Italy. I looked in both directions and saw no sign of life. I cut out a large section of the fence and crawled through. It seemed overly simple. I got to my feet in Italy, flipped the pliers back into France, and looked around vacantly, waiting for whistles to blow or sirens to sound or bullets to whine overhead. Nothing happened. I turned, finally, and walked on into Italy.

121

•   •   •

A farmer in a light pickup truck drove me as far as Torino, where I caught a train to Milan. With Mussolini gone, the Italian trains no longer ran on time. Mine was an hour late leaving Torino and lost another hour on the way to Milan. I left it in Milan and thought about buying a car. I had no contacts in Italy that lay anywhere near my route to Udine near the Yugoslav border. A secondhand Fiat would cut the distance and might be safer. I could drive without stopping and no one would notice my face, as might happen on a train.

But did one need a driver's license to purchase a car? I was not sure. I found a dealer's lot on the northern outskirts of Milan and looked at several cars. The cheapest was 175,000 lire, a little less than three hundred dollars. I could afford to pay for it in Swiss francs. I presented my Swiss passport as identification, and the dealer took it into the shop with him. I patted the little Fiat on the fender. With luck, I thought, the car could be a tremendous asset. I would have the registration and the passport and I might be able to drive it right across the Yugoslav border without any difficulty. That would cut down the risk considerably, leaving me only one tricky border to cross—the one into Turkey. And by that time I would be able to think of something. I was sure of it.

But the dealer seemed to be taking an unduly long time with my passport. I walked over to the office and saw him crouched over his desk, talking on the telephone.

There was something furtive in his manner. I moved closer and caught a few words. "Swiss passport...Henri Boehm...the one you are looking for, the fugitive—"

I ran like a thief.

122

. . .

In downtown Milan I picked up a copy of the Paris edition of the *New York Herald Tribune* and learned what all the fuss was about. The passports were a dead issue, worthless now, a liability. Someone had connected me to the tall man who had been shot down in Dublin. The paper didn't spell it out but explained that the fugitive Evan Michael Tanner had stolen important government documents in Ireland and was thought to be making his escape through continental Europe. They knew I had left Dublin under the false American passport and knew I had changed money under the British one at Madrid.

In an alleyway I destroyed the other two passports. I broke the cases open, tore the printed matter into scraps, and tossed the scraps to the winds. I was about to do the same to the remaining passport, the one for Mustafa Ibn Ali, but it seemed to me that there might be a use for it sometime, perhaps in Yugoslavia. One never knew.

The newspaper article described the black attaché case I was carrying, so I had to rid myself of that, too. I didn't know where to throw it away, so I sold it in a secondhand store for a handful of lire. The money was scarcely enough to matter, but I was getting to the point where money mattered, even small amounts. The damned car dealer still had my Swiss francs, and I was starting to run out of cash.

I buttoned under my shirt the packet of papers I had taken from the attaché case and walked to the railroad station. Would they be watching it? I had no doubt that they would. They had had a call from the car dealer, and I had confirmed his suspicions by bolting like a bat out of hell. I stopped on the way and bought a change of clothes, a hat, heavy shoes. At least I no longer matched the description the dealer would have given them.

I caught a train for Venice without incident. I bought my ticket on the train, locked myself in my compartment and read the rest of the *Herald Tribune*. The sky was dark by the time we reached Venice. I was glad of this. I felt safer in the dark, less conspicuous.

Another bus took me northeast to Udine. I felt as though I had been traveling forever, moving endlessly and to no great purpose. Plane, bus, train, hay wagon, train, bus, car, truck, train, bus—I wondered why I hadn't flown from Dublin to Venice in the first place and cut out all the island-hopping in between. The answer, of course, was that I had wanted to get out of Dublin as quickly as possible. But I seemed to be doing everything wrong. I had put them on my trail all over again by stupidly flashing the Swiss passport in Milan. They probably realized I was on my way to Turkey. If nothing else, they obviously knew I was in Italy and would be able to guess that I was heading east.

And all I could do in the meanwhile was run from burrow to burrow like a frightened rabbit. I had the names of some Croat exiles in Udine, but I couldn't be sure they would help me. And if they did, what then? They could sneak me into Yugoslavia, and I could shuttle around from one band of Balkan conspirators to another. This time, though, I would be doing it all behind the Iron Curtain, where every third conspirator was an agent for the secret police.

Marvelous.

I wished, suddenly, that I could sleep. Just close my eyes and let everything go blank for a while. I had been running too long, I realized. I needed some time to let loose. That was one of the troubles with being able to live without sleep. Because one never got sleepy, one now and then failed to realize that one was tired. I had been going without any real rest since...when? Since the few hours of relative rest in the attic hideaway at the Dolans' house in Croom. And how long ago was that?

It was hard to calculate. It seemed as though the whole span of time was only one endless day, but that wasn't right. I'd been at the Dolans' one night, spent the next night skulking around Dublin waiting for the plane, spent the night after that waiting for Vicente to cut my throat in the hay cart, and now it was night again.

No wonder it was beginning to get to me.

Ljudevit Starcevic had a small farm outside of Udine. He grew vegetables, had a small grape arbor, and kept a herd of goats. When an independent Yugoslavia had been carved out of the Austro-Hungarian Empire at the close of the First World War, he had joined Stefan Radic's Croat Peasant Party. In 1925 Radic abandoned separatism and joined the central government. Starcevic did not. He and other Croatian extremists fought the central regime. Some were killed. Starcevic, who was very young at the time, was imprisoned, escaped, and eventually wound up in Italy.

He was astonished when I spoke to him in Croat.

He lived alone, he told me. His wife was dead, his children had married Italians and moved away. He lived with his goats and saw hardly anyone. And he wanted—desperately—to talk.

He fed me a dish of meat and rice. We sat together and drank plum brandy and talked of the future of Croatia.

"You have come from our homeland?"

"No," I said.

"You go there?"

125

"Yes."

"You must watch out for the Serbs. They are treacherous."

"I understand."

"How will you go?"

I explained that I had to cross the border. He wanted to know if I planned to start a revolution. It was difficult to keep from laughing aloud. There would never be a revolution, I was tempted to tell him. The little splinters of Balkan nationalism were almost entirely in exile, and the few who remained to plot and scheme against their governments were bent old men like Ljudevit Starcevic, himself.

But of course I did not say this. His was a noble madness and a special form of lunacy that I was happy to share with him. One may, in this happy world, believe what one wishes to believe. And it pleased me to believe that one day Croatia would throw off the yoke of the Belgrade Government and take her rightful place among the nations, just as it pleased me to believe that Prince Rupert would one day dispossess Betty Saxe-Coburg from Buckingham Palace, that the Irish Republican Army would liberate the Six Counties, that Cilician Armenia would be again reborn and, for that matter, that the earth was flat.

"I will not start a revolution," I said.

"Ah." His eyes were downcast.

"Not this time."

"But soon?"

"Perhaps."

His leathery face creased in a smile. "And now? What do you plan this trip, Vanec?"

"There are men I must see. Plans to be made."

"Ah."

"But first I must cross the border."

126

He thought this over for some time. "It is possible," he admitted. "I have been back myself. Not many times, you understand, because it is, of course, very dangerous for me. I am a hunted man in my native land. The police are constantly on the lookout for me. They know that I am dangerous. It would be death for me to be caught there."

It was entirely possible, I thought, that no one in the Yugoslav Government so much as knew his name.

"But I have been back. I go once in a very great while to see my people. It is a land of great beauty, my Croatia. But you know this, of course."

"Of course."

"But the border," he said, and put his face in his hands and closed his eyes in thought. "It is possible. I can take you myself. I am old, I move more slowly than I did in my youth, but it is no matter. I must take you, do you understand? Because there is no one else I could trust with the task!"

He stuffed tobacco into the bowl of a pipe and lit it with a wooden match. He puffed solemnly on the pipe, then set it down on the scarred wooden top of the table.

"I can take you," he said.

"Good."

"But not tonight. Not for several days. This is—what? Saturday night, yes?"

"Yes."

"Tomorrow is Sunday. That is no good. Then Monday, then Tuesday. Tuesday night will be good."

"It will?"

"Yes. Tuesday is the best night to cross the border. There is a stretch of the border just a few kilometers from here where there are three guards. Always three guards, walking back and forth. It is allowed to cross only at the Customs stations, you see. And at the rest of

127

the border where one is not allowed to cross there are always guards, and here there are three guards."

He relit the pipe. "But on Tuesday," he said triumphantly, "there will be only two guards!"

"Why is that so?"

"It is always so. Who knows why? Whenever I cross the border, I do so on Tuesday, Vanec."

"And on Tuesday—"

"On Tuesday two men must do the work of three. They cannot cover the space. Believe me, I know how to get you to Croatia. My only worry is your fate when you arrive. Never trust the Serbs. Trust a snake before a Serb, do you follow me?"

I didn't entirely, but I said I did.

"But tonight is Saturday," said Ljudevit Starcevic. "Saturday, Sunday, Monday, Tuesday. You must stay here until then. It will be easy for you. It will be safe here. Who would look for you here? No one. You will eat, you will sleep, you will walk in the fields with the goats and sit with me by the fire. Do you play dominoes?"

"Yes."

"Then we will play dominoes. And you will get as much rest as possible so that you will be fresh and at ease when it is time for you to return to our homeland."

Saturday, Sunday, Monday, Tuesday. I would have to stay in one place all that time, marking time when I might otherwise be working my way inch by inch through Yugoslavia and into Turkey. For all those vital days I would be stuck on a farm in the northeast corner of Italy with nothing to do but eat and drink and rest and read and play dominoes.

It sounded wonderful.

12

Clouds filled the sky all Tuesday afternoon. The night was black as a coal mine, moonless and starless. Around eight o'clock old Starcevic and I set out for the border. I carried a leather satchel he had given me. In it was a loaf of bread, several wedges of ripe cheese, a flask of plum brandy, and the inevitable mysterious documents that were my last souvenir of Ireland. We walked along narrow mountain paths. There was lightning and thunder in the west, but the storm was a long way off, and it was not raining where we were.

When we approached the border, Starcevic drew me down in a clump of shrubbery. "Now we must be very quiet," he whispered. "In a few moments the border guard will pass us. You see that tree? If you climb it, you can get over the fence. I have climbed it and I am an old man, so you will be over it with no difficulty. We will wait until the guard passes and then we will wait five minutes, no longer, and then you will climb the tree and jump over the fence. It is not Croatia on the other side, you know. It is Slovenia."

"I know."

"Trust a snake before a Slovene. Tell them nothing. But in Croatia you will meet your friends."

"Of course."

"But why do I tell you these things?" He laughed softly. "You could tell me more than I could tell you, for it is you who will start the revolution."

"I—"

"Oh, I know, I know. You must not say as much, not even to me. But I know, Vanec. I know."

He fell silent. I waited, my eyes on the tree and the fence beyond it. The tree did not look all that easy to climb. There was a branch that extended over the fence, and I saw that it would be possible to move along the branch and jump clear of the fence. It would also be possible to make a very attractive target on the branch, outlined against the sky. At least the sky was dark and, according to Starcevic, there would be worlds of time once the sentry had passed.

After a few moments we saw the sentry pass. He was tall enough to play professional basketball. He wore high laced boots and a severely tailored uniform and carried a rifle. In my mind I saw him swing the rifle surely and easily, like a gunner in a movie short on skeet-shooting, zeroing in on a man poised on the branch of a tree, squeezing off an easy shot and dropping his prey.

We waited five long minutes. Then Starcevic touched my shoulder and pointed at the tree. I ran to it, tossed my leather satchel high over the fence, and shinnied up the tree. I climbed out onto the proper branch and felt it bend under my weight, but it held me, and I moved out until I was clear of the boundary fence. I had the horrible feeling that a gun barrel was trained on me and I waited

130

for a shot to pierce the night. No shot came. I caught hold of the branch with my hands, let my feet swing down, then let go and dropped a few yards to the ground. I found the satchel, snatched it up, and started walking.

So that was the Iron Curtain, I thought. A stretch of barbed wire one could pass over simply by shinnying up a tree. A hazardous obstacle for James Bond and his cohorts but child's play for that great Croatian revolutionary, Evan Tanner.

I felt wonderful. The days and nights at Starcevic's farm had done me worlds of good. Merely staying in one place for a few days rested me, and the security of knowing that I was safe, that I could eat and drink and lie down without constantly looking over my shoulder for police in one shape or another was a luxury to which I had recently become unaccustomed. Starcevic himself was a decent enough companion, pleasant enough to talk with and agreeably silent when I did not feel like talking. He worried that I was not getting enough sleep, as I always stayed up after he went to bed and managed to be awake before he rose in the morning. But he was so happy to have someone around to speak Croat to him and play dominoes with him that he was careful not to press or pry.

Now, rested and recovered, I felt equal to the challenge of Yugoslavia. It could be both easy and hard at once; it was a police state, on the one hand, and it was at the same time an utter gold mine of political extremists. The national groups that made up Yugoslavia were by no means a homogenized blend. Each province had dreams of independence, and in each province there were men whom I knew, men to whom I had written those cryptic notes. It was easy to construct a route that would lead safely and surely down into Bulgaria and from there to Turkey. I had entered Slovenia. I would move south and east through Croatia and Slavonia to Vukovar on the Danube—where I was awaited—then south through Serbia, stopping in Kragujevac, and on to Djakovica in Kosovo-Metohija, and stopping finally in any of several towns in Macedonia before turning east for the Bulgarian border. The whole trip would run around five hundred miles, and I might have to take my time, but I could expect to be sheltered every step of the way.

And there would be no Estebans in Yugoslavia, no inept conspirators. An inept conspirator in Yugoslavia very speedily found his way into prison. These men of mine might lead equally futile lives, but they would be professionals in their futility. I could count on them.

By dawn Wednesday I had reached the Slovenian city of Ljubljana. There a displaced Serbian teacher took me into his house, fed me breakfast, and took me to a friend who let me ride to Zagreb in the back of his truck. The ride was bumpy but quick. In Zagreb, Sandor Kofalic fed me roasted lamb and locked me in his cellar with a bottle of sweet wine while he rounded up a Croat separatist who had landed a berth as a minor functionary in the local Communist Party. I never learned the man's name; he didn't mention it, and I had the sense not to ask it. He provided me with a travel pass that would let me ride the trains as far as Belgrade (bypassing Vukovar). I would have to be careful in Belgrade, he counseled me, and I should not attempt to take the trains any further south, but, if I had friends, I would find my way readily enough.

In Belgrade I had dinner with Janos Papilov. He did not have a car, he told me, but a friend of his did, and perhaps he could borrow it. I waited at his house and played cards with his wife and father-in-law while he went to hunt up transportation. He came back with a car, and late at night we set out. He drove me sixty miles to Kragujevac and apologized that he could go no farther. Like the others I had met, he did not ask where I was going or why I was going there. He knew only that I was a comrade and in trouble and assumed that I was going someplace important and had something important to do there. That was enough to satisfy him.

I stayed the night in Kragujevac with an old widow who had a son in America. She told me that much and nothing more, asked no questions, and told me to keep away from the windows. I did this. In the morning, before the sky was light, I left her house and walked south on a road out of town. The woman had no transportation available and was unable to arrange any for me, so I took the road south, picked up a ride with a farmer as far as the little town of Kraljevo, and there caught up with a neat relay network that took me step-by-step down to Djakovica. Nine men combined to carry me a little over a hundred miles. Each took me ten or twelve or fifteen miles on horseback, turned me over to yet another man, and returned home.

By nightfall I was in Tetovo in Macedonia. And there I felt safer than ever. The whole province of Macedonia is peppered with revolutionaries and conspirators. The ghost of the IMRO, the Internal Macedonian Revolutionary Organization, had never been entirely laid. In the years before the First World War the IMRO had its own underground government in the Macedonian hills, ran its own law courts, and dispensed its own revolutionary justice. Its spies and agents ran amok throughout the Balkans. And, though generations have passed since the cry of "Macedonia for the Macedonians" first echoed through that rocky would-be nation, the IMRO lives on. It may be found in every hamlet of Macedonia. It is listed even now on the U.S. attorney general's list of subversive organizations.

Of course I am a member.

In Tetovo I stopped at a café for a glass of resinous wine. I had gradually changed my clothing in the course of my pilgrimage through Yugoslavia, and I was now wearing the same sort of garb as most of the men in the café. I received a few glances, perhaps because I was a stranger, but no one paid much attention to me. I drank the wine, asked directions to the address I had, and headed for Todor Prolov's house.

It was a smallish hut at the end of a drab and narrow street off the main thoroughfare, on the southeast edge of downtown Tetovo. Broken panes of glass in the casement windows had been patched with newspaper. Two dogs, thin and yellow-eyed, slept in the doorway and ignored me.

I knocked at the door.

The girl who opened the door had an opulent body and blonde hair like spun silk. She held a chicken bone in one hand.

"Does Todor Prolov live here?"

She nodded.

"I wrote him a letter," I said. "My name is Ferenc."

Her eyes, large and round to begin with, now turned to saucers. She grabbed my arm, pulled me inside. "Todor," she shouted, "he is here! The one who wrote you! Ferenc! The American!"

A horde of people clustered around me. From the center of the mob, Todor Prolov pushed forward to face me. He was a short man with a twisted face and unruly brown hair and a pair of shoulders like the entire defensive line of the Green Bay Packers. He reached out both hands and gripped my upper arms. When he spoke, he shouted.

"You wrote me a letter?" he bellowed.

"Yes."

"Signed Ferenc?"

"Yes."

"But you are Tanner! Evan Tanner!"

"Yes."

"From America?"

"Yes."

A murmur of excitement ran through the group around us. Todor released my arms, stepped back, studied me, then moved closer again.

"We have been waiting for you," he said. "Ever since your letter arrived, all of Tetovo has been in a state of excitement. Excitement!"

Again his hands fastened on my biceps. "And now the big question," he roared. "Are you with us?"

"Of course," I said, puzzled.

"With IMRO?"

"Of course."

He stepped forward and caught me in a bear hug, lifting me up off my feet and leaving me quite breathless. He set me down, spun around, and shouted at the crowd.

"America is with us!" he roared. "You have heard him speak, have you not? America will aid us! America supports Macedonia for the Macedonians! America will help us crush the tyranny of the Belgrade dictatorship! America backs our cause! America knows our history of resistance to oppression! America is with us!"

Behind me the streets had suddenly filled up with Macedonians. I saw men holding guns and women with bricks and pitchforks. Everyone was shouting.

"The time has come!" Todor shrieked. "Raise the barricades! March on the homes of the tyrants! Root out and destroy the oppressors! Give no quarter! Rise and die for Macedonia!"

A child rushed by me holding a bottle in his hand. There was a rag stuffed into the neck of it. The rag smelled of gasoline.

I turned to the girl who had opened the door for me. "What's happening? What's going on?"

"But of course you know. You are a part of it."

"A part of what?"

She hugged me with joy. "A part of our triumph," she said. "A part of our finest hour. A part of—"

"What?"

"Our revolution," she said.

13

The street had gone mad. There were so many guns going off that they no longer sounded like gunfire. It was too much to be real, more like a fireworks display on the Fourth of July. To the north a row of houses was already in flames. A police car roared past us, and men dropped to their knees to fire at it. One shot burst a tire. The car swung out of control, plowed off the street into a shop front. The police jumped out, guns ready, and the men in the street shot them down.

The girl was at my side. "They're crazy," I said. "They'll all be killed."

"Those who die will die in glory."

"They can't stand off an army—"

"But America will help us."

I stared at her.

"You said America would help. You told Todor—"

"I told him I was behind his cause. That is all."

"But you are with the CIA, are you not?"

"I'm *running from* the CIA."

"Then, who will help my people?"

"I don't know."

Two blocks down the street a canvas-topped truck careened around the corner and pulled to a stop. Uniformed troops spilled from it. Some of them had machine guns. They crouched at the side of the truck and began firing into the crowd of Macedonians. I saw a woman cut in two by machine-gun fire. She fell, and a baby tumbled from her arms, and another blast of gunfire tore the child's head off.

Shrieking, a young girl heaved a homemade cannister bomb into the nest of soldiers. The gunfire ceased. Two of the soldiers staggered free of the truck, clutching at their wounds, and a ragged volley of shots from the rooftops cut them down.

Sirens blared to the north. The whole town was alive with the fury of the uprising. The girl was still at my side, but I wasn't paying attention to the words she said.

Revolution—

I had told Starcevic there would be no revolution. Not in his beloved Croatia, not anywhere. I was, after all, no revolutionary, no *agent provocateur*. I was simply a treasure hunter headed for a cache of gold. But it was I who had sparked this, and it was, after all, a revolution. Mills bombs, Molotov cocktails, barricades thrown up in the streets, bursts of gunfire, the screams of the wounded—these were not sound effects, not bits of the backdrop of a movie, but the sounds of a popular rising, a revolution.

When one has long been conditioned to respond in a certain fashion to a certain set of stimuli, one does not think things out. One reacts and glories in it.

I reacted.

A police van had piled up at the barricade closing the south end of the block. A trio of uniformed troopers

138

had taken up positions behind the barricade and were firing at us. Two had rifles, one a Sten gun. I grabbed up a brick from the ground and heaved it at them. It fell far short.

Their fire came our way. I ran forward, toward the source of the firing. A youth ran beside me, pistol in hand. More shots rang out. The youth dropped, moaning, wounded in the thigh.

I grabbed up his pistol.

I kept running. The Sten gun swung around and pointed at me. I fired without aiming and was astonished to see the policeman spill forward, a massive hole in his throat. His blood washed out of him and coated the piled-up bedsteads and furniture of the improvised barricade. One of the other police fired at me. The bullet brushed my jacket. I ran toward him and shot him in the chest. The third one shoved a rifle in my face and pulled the trigger. The gun jammed. I clubbed him aside and kicked him in the face. He was reaching for another gun when I lowered the pistol and blew off the back of his head.

A cheer went up behind me. The rebels had fired a public building in the center of town. I grabbed up the Sten gun of the first cop I had killed and pushed forward with the crowd. For four blocks almost every house we passed was in flames. In the middle of the city, we pressed in around the police station. A small force of police and soldiers had barricaded themselves inside the stationhouse. They were firing into the crowd from the windows and lobbing grenades down amongst us. I saw the girl who had been at Todor's house putting a torch to the front door. The flames leaped. A band of men were heaving Molotov cocktails into a second-story window. The blaze spread in several places, and the crowd dropped back out of range to let the fire have its head.

We shot them down as they came out. There must

139

have been two dozen of them, not counting the ones who never got out the door.

In the public square, Todor proclaimed the Independent and Sovereign Republic of Macedonia. "Historic birthright" and "sever the shackles of Serbian oppression" were phrases that kept recurring. It was, all in all, a good proclamation. He paused once, and part of the crowd, thinking he had finished, began to cheer, but he picked up again, and the cheering died down. Then he did finish the speech, and a ground swell of exhilarated applause burst from the mass of people, and for a thin fraction of a moment I actually thought the revolution would succeed.

The Independent and Sovereign Republic of Macedonia, while unrecognized by the other independent and sovereign nations of the earth, did endure in fact for four hours, twenty-three minutes, and an indeterminate number of seconds. Thinking back, I cannot help viewing this lifespan as an enormous moral victory. It was at least five times the duration I would have predicted for the Republic, although it fell far short of Todor's expectations—he had announced at one point that Free Macedonia would endure, as was claimed for the Third Reich, for a minimum of a thousand years.

Those four hours were as active as any I had ever spent. After the police station fell to us, we still had to conduct mop-up operations throughout the town. It was necessary, for example, to dispatch a delegation to rouse the mayor from his bed, take him out of his house, and hang him from the tree in front of his front porch. It was also necessary to rush the town's small Serbian quarter and massacre the inhabitants thereof. I was fortunate enough to miss out on both the hanging and the pogrom, however. During this stage of the revolution I was cloistered with Todor and Annalya. Annalya was his sister, with blonde hair and huge eyes and hour-glass body. The three of us—a troika? a triumvirate? a junta? no matter— were to plan the course of the revolution.

"You shall not return to America," Todor insisted. "You shall stay here forever in Macedonia. I will make you my prime minister."

"Todor—"

"I will also make you my brother-in-law. You will marry Annalya. You like her?"

"Todor, what do we do when they send in the tanks?"

"What tanks?"

"They used tanks in Budapest in fifty-six. What can your people do against tanks?"

He thought this over. "What did they do in Budapest?"

"They used Molotov cocktails on them."

He brightened. "Then we will do the same!"

"It didn't work in Budapest. The revolt was crushed."

"Oh."

"The rebels were shot down by the hundreds. The leaders were executed."

While he tried to think of a reply to this dismal bit of news a man burst in with some information that took the edge off what I had said. Reports were coming in of sympathetic risings throughout Macedonia. Skopje, the provincial capital, was in flames. Kumanovo had gone to the rebels almost without a shot. There were rumors of rebellion in Britolj and Prilep in the south.

Todor rocked me with another bear hug. "You see? It is not one city in arms, like your Budapest. It is a nation taking its place among nations. It is an entire people rising as one man to throw off their chains and capture their freedom. And we shall triumph!"

Annalya and I left him. We ran around town, planning the defense of Tetovo. If it were true that other cities were in arms, we might have a little more time to prepare for the assault from Belgrade. We ranged barricades around the entire town, blocking off every road in and out of it and concentrating the bulk of our defenses across the main road in the north and the smaller roads immediately to either side of it. I was fairly certain the initial assault would come from that direction. If we were properly prepared, we might be able to break even in the first attack.

After that, when the tanks came down and the fighter planes dived overhead, was something I did not want to think about.

"Ferenc?"

"What?"

"Do we have any chance?"

I looked at her. I decided that she wanted me to lie to her, so I told her that there was a good chance we could win if every man fought as hard as he could.

"Ferenc?"

"What?"

"Tell me the truth."

"There is no chance, Annalya."

"I thought not. We will all be killed?"

"Perhaps. They may not want a massacre. The Russians got a fairly bad press after Hungary. They may just kill the leaders."

"Like Todor?"

I didn't answer her.

"It would be horrid if we lost and they spared him."

"I do not understand."

She smiled. "My brother wishes to be a hero. He is a hero already. He has fought like a hero and he will fight like a hero again when the troops arrive. It is only fitting that he die like a hero. Do you understand?"

"Yes."

"Where will the worst of the fighting be?"

"In the center."

"You are certain?"

I nodded. "The other streets are too narrow for heavy traffic. Even if they want to spread out for strategic reasons, the heavy weapons and the mass of men will come right down the center."

"Then I must be certain that Todor is here," she said. "In the center. May it please God that he dies before he learns that we are to be defeated."

I had spotters stationed a mile out on the main road to the north. When the revolution was just a hair under two hours old, they rode back full speed to announce that the troops were on their way. I asked what sort of vehicles were coming, but they had not noticed. In their eagerness to bring the news to us as fast as possible, they had neglected to determine just what sort of troops were headed our way or how many of them we could expect.

The first wave, as it turned out, was an afterthought. Evidently a mass of troops had been dispatched to the capital, and some major had decided it might be a good idea to find out what was happening in Tetovo. They sent four truckloads of infantry and two units of mobile artillery at us, and that wasn't enough to storm the city. We were properly deployed behind our barricades, we were fairly well armed, and we fought like cornered rats. The government troops threw everything they had at our center, and I told our men on the east and west to move in and engulf them.

We brought it off. The two small cannons never got to do us much damage. A batch of our sharpshooters

143

knocked off the two gun crews before more than four or five rounds had been fired, and the few shells that looped over the barricades at us had little effect. Bottles of flaming gas had the trucks in flames before the men had finished pouring out of them. We suffered casualties— over a dozen dead, almost as many wounded. But we completely destroyed the government forces.

Half an hour later they brought in an attacking force five times the strength of the first, and they rolled right over us.

14

Tetovo is one hundred twenty-five kilometers from the Bulgarian border. I crossed the border an hour before dawn in the locked trunk of a small gray two-door sedan that had been imperfectly manufactured in Czechoslovakia in 1959. In the front seat of the car were two IMRO members from Skopje. They crossed the border frequently and anticipated little trouble. The Bulgars, whatever their official position, had always been sympathetic to Macedonian separatism. The driver, a thickset, neckless man with two stainless steel teeth, insisted that our car would get only a cursory check at the border.

The other passenger was not so confident. The revolt, though history by then, would have put everybody on edge, he said, and the border officials would almost certainly insist on opening the trunk. He wanted me to ride beneath the rear seat, but I simply would not fit into that small space. So I wound up sitting in the trunk with a Sten gun across my knees, ready to start firing the minute the trunk opened.

When we stopped, a guard tapped on the trunk experimentally, then tried to open it. The driver gave him the key, but we had broken one of the teeth, and it didn't work. I heard two of the guards arguing. One insisted that they ought to shoot the lock off or at the very least pop the trunk open with a crowbar. The other, older and evidently more tired, said that he knew the driver, knew there was nothing in the trunk, and was not about to shoot up a man's car. For a while it looked as though the younger guard would get his way, and my finger was tight on the trigger, but finally they sent us on through.

We stopped a few miles from the border. The driver had a spare trunk key in reserve and let me out. I left him the Sten gun. We each had a drink of brandy, and he told me to take the flask along with me. I closed it and tucked it away in my leather satchel.

"You know where to go now, brother?"

"Yes."

"Good. Do not concern yourself for Annalya. She is safe, and we shall see that she is kept safe."

"Yes."

"And do not blame yourself for what has happened. Is that what you have been thinking? That it was your arrival that began the rising?"

"Perhaps."

"It would have come regardless. The time was right. Todor knew you brought no help from America. He used you, you see. Your coming was a sign, like a comet in the heavens. It fired the people and put steel in their courage. But there would have been a rising without you, although it would not have been so great a success."

"A success? We . . . your people . . . were butchered."

"Did you expect us to win?"

"No. Of course not."

146

"And did you think we were such fools that *we* expected victory?"

"But—"

"The reprisals will not be great. The Belgrade government is not that stupid. There will be concessions to us: perhaps a bit more autonomy, the removal of some of the more objectionable Serb ministers in Macedonia. That is one gain. And the other good result is just that action has been taken, that men have stood up and fought and died. A movement feeds on its own blood. Without nourishment it withers and dies. This has been a night of triumph, brother. We fought bravely, and you fought bravely with us. You are safe in Bulgaria?"

"Yes."

"You know the country?"

"I can get around well enough."

"Good. You are sure you do not wish the Sten gun?"

"It might be hard to explain if I get arrested."

"True. But handy in a corner, no? God protect you, brother. It was a good fight."

"It was."

I went eastward on foot, walking toward the emerging sun. The night had been very cold, but the morning was warm in the sunlight, the air very clean and fresh. The hillside was green, but a deeper and much darker green than the fields of Ireland. I was in no hurry and had no special fear of being noticed. My clothes were the same peasant gear worn by the men I saw working in their fields or walking along the road. I knew that they wanted me in Yugoslavia—the last moments in Tetovo, when Annalya and I had huddled together in the storm cellar waiting for a car to spirit us out of town, the army loudspeakers kept demanding that the villagers turn in the American spy. The Yugoslavs wanted me, and by now they might have a fair idea I had gone to Bulgaria, but I couldn't honestly believe they were on my trail. And the morning was too beautiful and the countryside too calming for me to be worried.

It was already growing difficult to believe that the revolution had really happened, that I had been in it and of it. For years I had read avidly of rebellions and coups and risings, of barricades in the streets and gunfire from the rooftops and homemade bombs and savagery and heroism and gutters awash with blood. I read contemporary accounts. I caught the flavor of what happened and what it was like. But it had always been something of which one read.

A girl I once knew took a trip to California and stopped to look at the Grand Canyon. Telling me of it, she said, "My God, Evan, you wouldn't believe it, it looks just like a movie." That, perhaps, is our framework of reference in today's world, our touch point for reality. Life is most lifelike when it best imitates art. The rising in Tetovo had been like a book or a movie, and already it was beginning to feel like something I had read or something I had watched upon a screen. Before that night I had fired guns only in the shooting gallery on Times Square. Now I had shot men and watched my bullets strike them and seen them die. There had, wondrously, been no sense of wonder at the time. And now I could barely believe what had occurred.

The major government assault on Tetovo had crushed our main force of defense and left Todor and a few dozen others dead at the onset. Then there was a stretch of time lost to memory, a confused and hectic bit of fearful scurrying. It never occurred to me to attempt to escape—

not, I think, because of a profound emotional commitment to our now-lost cause, but because I was too involved in the mechanics of the fighting, the regrouping of forces, the gunplay, the few pitiful defensive tactics of which we were still capable. It was Annalya who decided that I had to escape and who dragged me away from the fighting, brought me and my leather satchel to relative safety in the cellar, and finally got us a ride south and east of Tetovo.

"You wanted to make sure your brother was killed," I said. "Why are you making sure that I get away?"

"For the same reason."

"I don't understand."

"Todor had to die in battle," she said. "And you must escape. It would be bad for us if the enemy captured you. This way you are our American, mysterious, romantic. The government will know you were here with us and will be unable to lay hands on you. And our people will know you will return some day and resume the fight. So you must escape."

She accompanied me to the farmhouse but refused to go to Bulgaria with me. She felt she would be safe where she was and that she could not leave her people. Her place, she said, was with them. And, in that farmhouse, while other men drank bitter coffee in the kitchen, she asked me to go upstairs with her and make love to her. In a passionless voice she at once offered herself and insisted that her offer be accepted.

It was both loving and loveless—and better than I had thought it would be. Until the moment our bodies joined, it was impossible to think of the act, let alone experience anything resembling desire. But then I was astonished by the urgency of it all. And I was more astonished yet at her cries at a moment of what might

149

have been passion. "A son! Give me a son for Macedonia!"

I did my best.

It took quite a while to reach Sofia, but the city held refuge for me. My host, a priest in the Greek Orthodox Church, lived on the Street of the Tanners, appropriately enough. I did not point out this coincidence to him since I did not tell him my name. I was sent to him by an IMRO member who was also a member of an organization called the Society of the Left Hand. I had heard of this group before but knew very little about it. It seemed to be a quasi-mystic band organized centuries ago to preserve Christianity in the Ottoman Empire. For a time, in the late nineteenth century, they may have engaged in terrorism for profit. I had read that the group had long since ceased to exist, but one learns to disregard such incidental intelligence. Like Mark Twain's obituary, the death notices of extremist groups are often somewhat premature.

And yet, my lack of knowledge of the Society of the Left Hand greatly inhibited conversation. I dared not espouse any particular political viewpoint lest it should develop that Father Gregor did not happen to be in sympathy with that point of view. My IMRO friend had scheduled an eight-hour stay at Father Gregor's for me, after which time I would be able to ride south toward the Turkish border with another friend of his. The first hours passed easily enough. Father Gregor's housekeeper produced an excellent shashlik, and his cellar yielded up a commendable bottle of Tokay. Afterward we sat in his parlor and played chess. His game was better than mine, so much so that we stopped after three games; it was clearly no contest.

150

As he returned the chessmen to their box he asked if I by any chance spoke English. "I would welcome the chance to speak that language," he said. "One requires frequent practice to remain fluent in a tongue, and I have little opportunity to practice English."

"I have some English, Father Gregor, and would be pleased to converse with you in English."

"Ah, it is good. More wine?" He refilled our glasses. "In an hour we shall have a treat. Or perhaps I should say that you will share my daily treat, if it is your pleasure. At nine o'clock there is a broadcast of Radio Free Europe. Do you often hear it?"

"No."

"For my part, I never miss it. And just as that program concludes there is a broadcast of Radio Moscow, also beamed to Sofia. This is another program I always enjoy hearing. Do you listen to Radio Moscow?"

"Not often."

"Ah. Then, I think it shall be a treat for you. The juxtaposition of these two radio programs is a delight to me. One is dashed from one world to another, and neither of the two worlds reflected has much in common with the world one sees from Sofia. Is this your first visit to Sofia?"

"Yes."

"It is a pity you cannot spend more time here. The city has charms, you know. One thinks of Bulgaria as a crude simple nation of peasants milking their goats and eating their yogurt and living a hundred years or more. One never calls to mind the striking architecture of Sofia or the busy commercial life in the city. I was born on a farm not ten miles from this city and have spent most of my life here. But I have traveled a bit. During the war it was wise to travel. One perhaps was better off if one did not spend all one's time in one place. Do you have difficulty understanding my English?"

"No. You speak very well."

"I was in London for a time. Also in Paris and for a short time in Antwerp. When the time seemed propitious I returned to Sofia. Many of my closest associates have questioned my decision to return here. Why, they wondered, would I elect to spend the remainder of my life in a solemn and often joyless Balkan city? Perhaps you ask yourself the same question."

I attempted something noncommittal.

"One discovers," he said, "that one place is rather like another. And that one's own home, one's ancestral home, has something special to recommend it. You go to Turkey from here, is that correct?"

"Yes."

"To any particular city?"

"Ankara."

"Ah, yes. I was there once many years ago, but I remember very little of the city. My own position then was similar to yours now in Sofia. I had the opportunity to visit the city but lacked the chance to tour it, to see something of its sights. It is unfortunate, I would say, that the involved man has no time for sightseeing. While the tourist, on the other hand, can examine areas at his leisure but cannot relate them to himself because they are not truly involved in his pattern of life. Would you agree?"

I agreed. And I thought specifically of my tour of Andorra, traversing the tiny republic beneath a load of hay. *The involved man—*

By the time we were ready to listen to Radio Free Europe, I still had learned no more of the nature of the Society of the Left Hand. We sat in his library, surrounded by four walls of books, while he fiddled with the dials of an antiquated short-wave radio. I thought of the U.S. television commercials, peasant families huddled together in the darkness, the radio pitched low, the listeners keeping one ear on the voice of freedom and the other ear tuned in anticipation of a knock on the door, a visit from the secret police, a beating, a forced confession, a bullet fired point-blank into the back of the neck. In our comfortable chairs, sipping our large glasses of Tokay, that particular commercial seemed violently unreal.

Throughout the program Father Gregor kept giving vent to peals of unrestrained laughter. He was a tall man, a heavy man, and when he laughed, the walls shook. "Marvelous," he would roar. "Extraordinary," he would explode. And the room would rock with his laughter.

Two news items, both delivered fairly late in the hour, were of special interest to me.

The first was a straightforward report on the revolution in Macedonia. "Do not despair, freedom-lovers of Bulgaria," said the intense voice of a young woman. "The spirit of independence cannot be ground out beneath the heel of communism. Last night patriots in Macedonia rose up in open rebellion against the so-called People's Republic of Yugoslavia. Fighting with sticks and stones, men and women and children stood up on their feet and cast off their chains, fighting against insuperable odds to free themselves from the shackles of economic slavery." The voice dropped an octave. "And once more the brute force of the tyrant crushed the spark of rebellion. Once more the Beast of Budapest trampled on the hope of a people. Once more blood ran red in the streets of yet another country wedged in the shadow of the Russian bear." The voice reasserted itself. "Europeans, Free Europeans, take heart from the example of these Macedonian heroes! The soil of liberty is fertilized anew by their blood! They have not died in vain! Your day—the day of all mankind—shall come!"

Father Gregor laughed and laughed.

Later in the same program I heard my own name mentioned. I almost dropped my wine glass. This time the speaker was male.

"Yet another act of Russian provocation has threatened the peace of the world," the announcer proclaimed. "This time the crime is espionage, a black art that seems to have been invented in Moscow. The criminal band operates under the leadership of Evan Michael Tanner, an American citizen corrupted by the communist lies and tainted by communist bribery. Through stealth and subterfuge this traitor to the peace of the world managed to get hold of the complete dossier of the British air and coastal defenses. The key defense secrets of this gallant European nation are even this minute moving behind the Iron Curtain toward the tyrant's home base in Moscow.

"Yet there is still hope for mankind. Tanner, it has been learned, is on his way to a small city in northwestern Turkey, there to make contact with his superiors. Will he be intercepted? Free men everywhere, peace-loving men throughout the world, can only pray that he will . . ."

There was a further denunciation of Russian espionage, but I barely heard it. My head was spinning, my palms dotted with sweat. I stole a look at Father Gregor. He seemed too absorbed in the program to pay any attention to me. He was laughing frequently now.

British air and coastal defenses—but how could they have been stolen in Ireland? And if they had been stolen in England, why on earth would the tall man have run to Ireland with them? And for whom had he been working? And why? And—

Gradually, as the announcer shifted to another point,

154

I managed to work out at least a part of it. The only way it made any sense was that the Irish themselves had stolen the British plans. Then the tall man or some other member of his gang had filched the plans a second time in Dublin. That would explain why it was the gardai rather than some branch of British Intelligence that had picked up the tall man's trail, arrested him, and eventually shot him dead.

Who he might be and who might be his employers were still unanswerable questions. But they did not matter tremendously. What did matter was that I seemed to have a load of dynamite in my little leather satchel. It scarcely concerned me where the plans had come from or where they were supposed to be going. But the whole world now knew that I had those plans and the whole world also knew, somehow, that I was on my way to Balikesir, and this was a matter of considerable concern.

How they had found out was another good question. Any of several persons could have told them—Kitty, the Dolans, even Esteban, although I couldn't recall mentioning my precise destination to him. For that matter, I had left a map of Turkey in my apartment, with Balikesir circled in bright blue ink. By now it was reasonable to assume that my apartment had been searched a dozen times over, and the bright blue circle on my map would certainly have been noticed by someone. I didn't think Kitty would have talked and I couldn't picture the Dolans as informers, but of course if Esteban had known anything I'm sure he would have run off at the mouth to the first person who caught hold of him.

The Radio Moscow program had an added kicker. Nothing about the British plans this time, nothing at all. But there was a brief report that went something like this:

"Continuing their program of harassment, agents of

the American Central Intelligence Agency once again launched a desperate attempt to undermine the security of one of the peace-loving socialist republics of Eastern Europe. This time our sister nation of Yugoslavia was the victim. Playing on racial friction and decadent economic drives, CIA operatives under the direction of Ivan Mikhail Tanner sparked an abortive fascist coup in the Province of Macedonia. With tons of smuggled weapons and the tactics of Washington-trained terrorists, these social fascists were able to overcome the efforts of the fine people of several Macedonian villages. Through the efforts of people in the surrounding territory, and with the aid of crack government troops from Belgrade, the Washington-inspired uprising was quickly brought under control and the wave of terror ended forever."

I poured myself a fresh glass of wine. It was beginning to look as though there would be quite a delegation waiting for me in Balikesir. The British, the Irish, the Russians, the Turks, the Americans—and, of course, the nameless band that had stolen those plans in the first place.

Why, I was finally beginning to wonder, hadn't I stayed home where I belonged?

"Perhaps I am overly fond of those two programs," Father Gregor commented. "Each, as you can see, is a source of great amusement to me. You noticed, for example, the two rather divergent views of last night's trouble in Macedonia? I wonder which came closest to the truth."

We were drinking thick, bitter coffee in small cups. The radio was silent now. I had trouble paying attention to Father Gregor. My mind was grimly occupied with two problems—the impossibility of entering Turkey and the equal impossibility of leaving Turkey.

156

"I noticed, too, that one man was mentioned on both programs, though in different contexts. A Mr. Tanner. Did you notice that?"

"Yes."

"Do you find this amusing?"

"I—"

He smiled gently. "May we halt this masquerade? Unless I am very much mistaken, which, I admit, is of course a possibility, I believe that you are the Evan Michael Tanner of whom they speak. Is that correct?"

I didn't say anything.

His eyes glinted brightly. "The infinite variety of life, Mr. Tanner. Once, shortly after the war, I had two alternative courses of action. I could continue to lead a very fast-paced absorbing life. Or I could, so to speak, retire to Sofia. I selected the latter course. As I've mentioned, many persons questioned this decision. That American song—how does it go? About the difficulty of keeping boys on the farm after they've been to France. Do I have it right?"

"More or less."

"Good. At any rate, I made my decision. The precise reasons for it are unimportant. A combination, perhaps, of self-preservation and the conservatism that comes with years. I have noticed, though, that life does not pass one by. When one lives in Sofia, excitement comes to Sofia."

He picked up his coffee, studied it, then set the cup down untasted. "I suspected your identity from the first, if you are interested. You were referred by a member of IMRO, and of course that made me think of Macedonia, and I had heard of you in connection with the uprising. And we spoke in English. That was a test of mine, you see. Your Bulgar is better than my own English, actually. Quite unaccented. But your English has an American accent. This led me to the rather obvious conclusion that you were an American. And during the program I observed your reactions to the various reports upon your activities. But you do not really want to hear me boast of my prowess as a detective, do you? Hardly. At any rate, I know that you are you. Are you really going to Ankara? Or was the report correct?"

"I'm going to a small town. As they said."

"Ah. You have friends there?"

"No."

"None at all?"

"None."

He stroked his chin. "I trust you have a very important reason for going there?"

"Yes."

"May I ask you a delicate question?"

"Of course."

"You need not answer it, and I need not add that you have the option to answer it untruthfully. Is there, perhaps, the opportunity for you of financial profit in Turkey?"

I hesitated for some time. He waited in respectful silence. Finally I said that there was an opportunity for financial profit.

"Substantial profit?"

"Quite."

"So I suspected. I presume you would prefer not to tell me your precise destination in Turkey?"

Did it matter? The rest of the world already seemed to know. I said, "Balikesir."

"I do not know it. In the northwest?"

"Yes."

He took an atlas from a shelf, thumbed through it, located a map of Turkey, studied it, then looked up at me and nodded. "Balikesir," he said.

"Yes."

Father Gregor got to his feet and walked to the window. While looking out it he said, "In your position, Mr. Tanner, I would have a great advantage. I am, as you no doubt know, of the Left Hand. I would be able to enlist the aid of other members of the Left Hand. If I were attempting to bring something into Turkey, they might help me. If, on the other hand, I were bringing something out of Turkey, they again might be of assistance."

I said nothing. I sipped my coffee. It was cold.

"Of course, there is a custom in the Society. I would be expected to give to the Left Hand a tithe of the proceeds of the venture. A tenth part of whatever gain I realized."

"I see."

"What sort of profit do you anticipate?"

"Perhaps a great deal if my information is correct. Perhaps none at all."

"How large a sum if your information is right?"

I named a figure.

"A tenth part of that," said Father Gregor, "would be a substantial sum. Sufficient, I am sure, to interest the Left Hand."

I said nothing.

"But perhaps you would not care to part with a tithe?"

"That would depend."

"On whether you need assistance? And on whether it can be supplied?"

"More or less."

"Ah." He put his hands together. "It would be possible to assemble a dozen very skillful men in Balikesir at whatever time you might designate. It would be possible to supply the materials you might need for a proper escape. It would be possible—"

"A plane?"

159

"Not without extreme difficulty. Would a boat do?"

"Yes."

"A boat is easily arranged. How powerful a boat would you require?"

"One that could reach Lebanon."

"Ah. It is gold, then?"

"How did—"

"What else does one sell in Lebanon? For many items Lebanon is where one buys. But if one has gold to sell, one sells it in Lebanon. One does not get the four hundred Swiss francs per ounce one might realize in Macao, but neither does one get the one hundred thirty francs one would obtain at the official rate. I suspect you might realize two hundred fifty Swiss francs an ounce for your gold. Is that what you had anticipated?"

"For a priest," I said, "you're rather worldly."

He laughed happily. "There is only one thing."

"Yes."

"It would be necessary for you to join the Society of the Left Hand."

"I would have to become a member?"

"Yes. You are willing?"

"I know nothing about the Society."

He considered this for a few moments. "What must you know?"

"Its political aims."

"The Left Hand is above politics."

"Its general aims, then?"

"The good of its members."

"Its nature?"

"Secret."

"Its numerical strength?"

"Unknown."

"The nature of its membership?"

"Diverse and scattered throughout the earth. Largely

in the Balkans, but everywhere. Listen," he said, "you wish to know what you are joining. This is understandable. But you have no...what is the expression? Ah. You have no need to know. Perhaps I can tell you simply that my membership in the Left Hand enables me, a simple priest, to live quite nicely in a city where priests rarely live too well. Enough? And I might add that I have only been a priest for a handful of years at that. And that I have few priestly duties. You would be astonished to learn how long it has been since I have seen the inside of a church."

We sat looking at each other.

"You wish to join?"

"Yes."

"That is good." He went to another bookshelf, brought down a Bible, a ceremonial knife, and a piece of plain white cloth. I covered my head with the white cloth, gripped the knife in my right hand, and rested that hand atop the Bible.

"Now," said Father Gregor, "raise your left hand..."

15

I entered Balikesir three days later on the back of a
toothless donkey. From the time I had left Father Gregor,
my journey had been an unceasing span of perilous mo-
notony. The trip from Sofia to the Turkish border was
uneventful. The crossing of the border, the most singularly dangerous border I had passed, was managed with
harrowing ease. With the British air and coastal defense
plans between my skin and my shirt, with the leather
satchel abandoned in Bulgaria, with my face unshaven
and my hair uncombed and my body unwashed, and with
Mustafa Ibn Ali's passport clenched in my sweaty hand,
I passed through Bulgarian exit inspection, Turkish en-
trance inspection, and on into Turkey. As I took my first
steps onto Turkish soil a whistle sounded to my rear,
and someone began shouting. I very nearly broke into a
run. It was well that I did not. The whistle and shouting
were not for me, after all, but for some fool who had
walked away without his suitcase.

After I had bought the donkey, I had just a handful

of change left for food. The donkey and I worked our way south and west past Gallipoli and crossed the Dardanelles on the ferry *Kilitbahir* to Canakkale. Then we proceeded southeast to Balikesir. I had to stop from time to time to feed the poor animal and let him get some sleep. As we moved closer to our destination I had to stop even more often because one can ride a donkey only so long before one begins to yearn for a less punishing mode of transportation.

But such details are unimportant, even less exciting in the retelling than in the actual occurrence. I reached Balikesir in the early afternoon, hungry and nearly penniless. I sold the donkey for about a third of what I had paid for him and parted from him with the sincere wish that his next owner would use him more kindly and appreciate him more fully. I walked slowly but surely into the center of the city and knew at last how it felt to be at the eye of a hurricane.

For the remainder of the afternoon I wandered slowly through the downtown section. There could not possibly have been as many agents of various powers as I fancied I saw, but it certainly seemed as though the city was swarming with spies and secret agents of one sort or another. I heard men speaking Turkish in a wide variety of accents and tentatively identified three British operatives, two Irish, a batch of Americans, at least three Russians, and a slew of others whom I included in a broad category headed Spies—Allegiance Unknown.

I had to dodge them all. No one had taken the slightest notice of me yet, and I felt I could remain undetected indefinitely as long as I didn't do anything. But I also had to slip in and out of the streets of the city until I found that house high on a hill at the edge of town, the big house with the huge porch that Kitty Bazerian's grandmother may or may not have recalled correctly.

163

Then I had to break into the porch, remove the gold, accept help from the Society of the Left Hand, and, hardest of all, manage to avoid having the Left Hand walk off with every last cent of the proceeds.

Because I did not trust them an inch.

We had many grand plans, Father Gregor and I. A group of men were already finding their separate ways to Balikesir. We would meet there, according to his plans, and they would help me get the gold from Balikesir to a nearby port, probably Burhaniye. There a boat would lie at anchor, ready to take us on to Lebanon.

I believed this much. But I did not believe my brothers of the Left Hand would be content with a tenth portion. And I did not know how I could get to Beirut without their help, nor did I know how to accept their assistance without getting conned out of the whole treasure.

First things first. If I didn't find the house or if the house held no gold beneath its ample porch, I could forget the whole thing.

I almost hoped it would turn out that way.

There was a moon three-quarters full that night. Around nine I began hunting for the house, and it took me until an hour before dawn to find it. My mistake, at first, was in looking for a house near the edge of the city. What had been the edge of the city forty-odd years ago was the edge of the city no longer. I wasted a great deal of time learning this, then switched tactics and walked along the railroad bed looking for a house overlooking the tracks. It took time, a good deal of time, but it was there, and I found it.

Kitty's grandmother had given me a perfect description. The house was precisely as I had pictured it, large, towering over the houses on either side, with a huge porch with concrete sides. The rest of the house seemed an appendage of that porch, but that was no doubt attributable to my particular point of view.

The house needed painting badly. Some of its windows were broken, a few boards loose on its sides. I approached it very cautiously and came close enough for a quick examination of the porch. As far as I could tell, it had not been remodeled since 1922. The floorboards seemed to have remained undisturbed for a long period of time, and the concrete sides were uniformly black with age. There was one part where the porch might have been broken and recemented years ago—perhaps when the gold was originally hidden away there, or perhaps later when someone else had beaten me to the punch and removed the treasure. There was only one sure way to find out, and it was too close to dawn for me to make the attempt.

I drifted downtown again. I wasted the day wandering through the markets, killing time in a filthy movie house, sitting over cups of inky coffee in dark cafés. At night I returned to the house. I had purchased a crowbar at the market and had walked around all day with it hidden in the folds of my clothing. It would have been better in some ways to break in through the concrete, but I couldn't risk the noise and was afraid I would be unable to camouflage a hole in the concrete afterward.

I waited in the darkness until the last light went out in the huge old house. After another half hour, I went up onto the porch and worked at the boards with a crowbar. It was hellish work—I had to be silent, I had to be fast, and I had to be prepared to melt into the shadows at the approach of a car or a pedestrian. I pried loose boards in a corner of the porch where I hoped no one would be apt to step and finally cleared out a large enough area so that a man could slip through. I looked inside.

Naturally I couldn't see a thing. It was pitch dark within, and I hadn't had the sense to bring a torch.

The temptation to lower myself beneath the porch was overpowering. But it was already too late for safety, and I would have to figure out a way to close the hole after me if I wanted to go inside. I reached down, swung the crowbar down inside and touched nothing. If I just went inside for a moment or two—

Not without a light, I decided. I replaced the boards and fitted nails into enough of them so that no one would crash through, but left things sufficiently loose so that I could open up the hole again in a few minutes instead of a few hours.

Then I went back downtown to kill another day.

By the following night I had traded my crowbar for a small flashlight. I went back to the house—it felt like my home by now—and opened up the hole in the porch again. I had it open when I heard a car approach and I barely dropped from the porch and around the side of the house in time. The car was a police vehicle with a spotlight mounted on the fender. It slowed at the house, and the spotlight swung around onto the porch, and I believe I came very close to fainting. But they saw nothing but a few loose boards, and that was evidently not what they were looking for.

The car passed. I hurried back onto the porch, snapped on my pencil flash and aimed it down the hole in the floorboards into the dark area below the porch.

The beam it cast was weak. But it was enough. I was looking—wide-eyed, suddenly breathless—at the gold of Smyrna!

16

I spent the rest of the night beneath the porch. After I dropped through the opening, I arranged the floorboards carefully in place above me. I had to be reasonably quiet. A slight noise, even if heard, might be regarded as the movement of a rat, but repeated loud noises would be sure to attract attention. It was difficult to be silent at the beginning, however. I wanted to throw back my head and howl like a hyena. I had found the gold, and there was a hell of a lot of it, and it made a beautiful sight.

There were sacks and boxes and little leather purses, and everything was stuffed with gold coins. The great majority were British sovereigns with the head of Queen Victoria, but there was a scattering of Turkish pieces and a handful of pieces in each lot from other nations. Counting this treasure was out of the question. Instead, I incorporated the small bags inside the larger gunny sacks and tried to calculate the total weight of the treasure.

My guess placed it somewhere between 500 and 600 pounds. I tried to work out the value of the lot, but my mind would not behave properly. I got hung up on such points as whether to use the troy pound of twelve ounces or the avoirdupois pound of sixteen, whether to estimate on the basis of the official $35 per ounce or the $60-rate I was likely to get in Beirut. I decided ultimately that the whole question was academic. I was sitting in the exhilarating presence of somewhere around a quarter of a million dollars in gold. That was all I really had to know.

But how to get it out?

I hated the idea of a boat. The boat that Father Gregor's cohorts might supply would probably be capable of only twenty knots or so, and a trip from the west coast of Turkey all the way around to Lebanon would take days on end. Even a fast boat would be in the sitting-duck category, easy prey to the Turks whenever they got around to realizing who was on that boat.

A plane would simplify things. If the Society of the Left Hand were such a powerful organization, a plane should be obtainable. But I was beginning to feel more and more convinced that the Society of the Left Hand was very little more than the name of an elaborate confidence game and that the boat was going to take the gold right straight back to Bulgaria where Father Gregor would devise at his leisure a way to convey the gold to Lebanon, or to Macao, or wherever he happened to want it.

It might be best to avoid the Left Hand group entirely. But could I manage to get the gold out on my own? No, I could never bring it off. I had to use the Left Hand. And I also had to keep them from knowing what the right hand was doing.

• • •

The Society of the Left Hand made contact in the market a day later. A furtive little man with smallpox scars on his chin flashed me one of the secret signs—a particular arrangement of the fingers of the left hand that Father Gregor had taught me. I could have ignored him, as he did not seem all that confident that the ragged peasant before him was really the man he sought, but I knew I would need him, and it seemed pointless to be dodging everyone in Balikesir at once. I returned the sign. He nodded for me to follow him, and I did.

When we were clear of the crowd, he slowed down and permitted me to catch up with him. He gave me another sign, perhaps for insurance, and I made the appropriate countersign. Then he asked me who my father was. I said I had a father named Gregor. He smiled briefly and led me up one street and down another until we reached a large old house in the Arab section.

"We have rented this house," he said. "You will come inside?"

I went inside and met my four companions. There were three others, I was told. One waited in the harbor at Burhaniye with the boat they planned to use. Two others had left to make arrangements for a car. Had I found the gold? I said I had. Would we be able to get it out? I said we would.

They were all delighted.

"We will help you," the scarred one said. His name was Odon; the others had not volunteered their names. "And we will be content with a tenth of the proceeds."

He was the least convincing liar I had ever met in my life. If I had entertained any doubts as to their intentions—and in my wildly optimistic moments I had willed myself to believe Father Gregor's story—they were forever dispelled. There was now only one point that was unclear. I was unsure whether or not they would kill me after appropriating the gold for themselves.

"Where is the gold?"

I explained its approximate location.

"And how much is there?"

I told him my estimate.

"We will go tonight," Odon said. "There is no time to waste. We will go tonight in the car our men are obtaining. We will—"

"A stolen car?"

"We will purchase a car. One of our men has a Turkish driver's license and a passport to match it. There is no chance we will be questioned. We will go to the house and load the gold into metal strongboxes. You understand? We have the boxes in the garage. Come, I will show you."

There were two dozen steel strongboxes in the garage on top of a huge workbench. The bench overflowed with rusted hardware and tools—long rattail files, rusted padlocks, nuts, bolts, washers. Amid this sea of rusted metal the strongboxes gleamed brightly.

"Have we enough boxes?"

I calculated quickly. "Yes. They'll hold the gold."

"Good. We will fill them at the house. You understand? Or, for safety's sake, you will go beneath the porch and fill them. Then, when you are ready, the car will return for them, and we will all go at once to Burhaniye. Before dawn we will all be on our way." As an afterthought, and as further confirmation of the ship's true destination, he added, "To Beirut, of course. We will sail at once to Beirut."

A dismal liar.

• • •

That night clouds concealed the face of the moon. It was a bit of good luck. After midnight we drove to the house. Odon stayed in the car with two of the others. Another pair remained at the house—we were to stop for them before making the run to Burhaniye. I scurried onto the porch, opened up my little rabbit hole, and dropped down into my burrow. Another man passed the strongboxes down to me one at a time.

"Shall I wait with you?"

"No," I said. "Go back to the car. It will take me a while. Drive around or return to the house. Come for me in an hour."

He looked dubious. "I could come down there with you. It would go faster."

"We might be heard."

He went away. Eventually the car pulled off. I doubt that they all were in it. I'm fairly certain one stayed behind to make sure I did not attempt to get away with the gold.

I filled all twenty-four of the boxes. They were very heavy, but one could lift them without a great deal of trouble. I estimated each one weighed twenty-five or thirty pounds, which fitted with my original guess at the total weight of the treasure. I had finished packing the boxes by the time the car returned. Odon came to me from the car and suggested that I hand them up one at a time, and he would trek them back to the car.

That would make it a little too easy. I hopped out of my burrow. "I'm too exhausted to lift another thing," I said. "Send one of the other men to do the lifting. I'll wait in the car."

After all, there was no point in making it easy for them. I could picture them quite clearly, taking the last box from me, loading it into the trunk, and driving merrily away while I struggled out of the porch to wave bye-bye at them. No, I wouldn't be taken quite that easily.

I waited in the car. They brought the boxes out quickly enough, one man handing them up, two others relaying them to the car, Odon placing them in the trunk, but they made enough noise to wake corpses. Lights went on in the house across the way. I had visions of the whole thing going to hell in a handcar. I called to them to hurry, and they hurried, and they hurried, and lights went on in the house whose porch we were robbing. My head ached dully. My mouth was dry. We loaded the last box, and the men piled into the car. In the distance a siren howled. Police? Probably.

Odon started the engine. It didn't catch at first, and I was certain the idiot had flooded the motor. It caught the second time, and we got the hell out of there. He drove well, at least. He put the gas pedal on the floor, and we were back at home base in no time at all.

Odon stuck the car in the garage. "Get the others," he told one of the men. "And hurry. We have to be on that boat before dawn. There's no time."

I got out of the car. I passed the hardware bench, scooped off a curved linoleum knife. As I walked around the car I stuck the knife into the left rear tire, pulled it out fast, and pocketed it. The tire did not blow but went down fast, almost instantaneously. I let one of the others discover it. He pointed it out to Odon.

Odon cursed rather colorfully. Someone remembered that there was a spare in the trunk. He opened the trunk. The spare tire was wedged in behind the strongboxes. Three of us wrestled it out, and in the process I got in a few good licks with the linoleum knife. No one noticed these at first. They thought the tire merely needed to be inflated, and Odon discovered an air pump in the rear of the garage. The damned garage had everything. They

172

tried to pump up the tire, but it wouldn't inflate, and then the one who had passed me the strongboxes spotted the cuts in the tire and showed them to Odon, and Odon went out of his mind. He cursed the two who had purchased the car, cursed the fates for giving him fools for companions and threw in a few words that were not part of my command of Bulgarian.

He was obviously not at all pleased. "We have to get another car," he said. "Damn it to hell, somebody go out and steal a car. We have to—"

An argument developed. Two of the men utterly refused to make the trip in a stolen car. Another pointed out that they could get a tire in the morning and they could use some sleep for the time being.

"And if in the meanwhile someone runs off with the gold?"

"None but us know of it."

"And if one of us does so?"

"How? In a car with a flat tire?"

The wait-until-tomorrow crowd carried the day. Odon locked the trunk and closed the garage door. We all trooped inside the dingy house. A cupboard yielded up a bottle of rather poor brandy. We all drank, and Odon's spirits began to improve with drink. We drank and sang and drank and danced and drank, and one by one we dropped off to sleep until at last all of us were sleeping peacefully.

All but one of us.

When they were asleep, when it was as safe as it was likely to get, I slipped out of the house and into the garage. With such an abundant supply of tools around, the locked trunk was not much of an obstacle. I was very busy for almost an hour. Then I slipped back into the house. They were all still asleep.

I suppose the most intelligent move would have been

to murder them in their beds. I cannot honestly say that the thought did not occur to me. It did, and I felt foolish rejecting it out of hand, but I could not possibly have done otherwise.

I had killed men in Macedonia. I told myself as much, reminded myself that I had quite fiercely gunned down men who had done absolutely nothing to me, while I was now unable to kill a group of unpleasant men who intended to rob me blind. This did not seem to make any difference. The men I had killed in Macedonia had been gunned down in the heat of real or imagined revolutionary passion. It was quite a different matter to slash half a dozen throats in the dark of night. I was evidently incapable of it. And, actually, I was more than a little pleased by the discovery.

But I did not suspect my fellows shared my reservations regarding the murder of sleeping men. And so I contrived to be obviously awake before them. Odon sent a man out to buy a tire. He came back with it and put it on the car. There was another argument: Should we or should we not wait for darkness? We decided not to wait. Around two in the afternoon we all piled into the car and headed for Burhaniye.

It was an easy drive. The ship, a trim little cutter, lay at anchor, with a thickset man on board. He came down to greet us. The harbor officials were taken care of, he reported. They would look the other way. We need only load the ship and be off.

Odon took me aside. He handed me a sack full of padlocks. "You must lock the strongboxes," he said. "It is only fitting, as you are the man who will receive the greater share of the gold and you must be assured that we do not try to cheat you. If the boxes are not locked, we might take more than our share during the voyage. Do you understand?"

"But I trust you, Odon."

He very nearly blushed. "No matter," he said. "You take the boxes from the trunk. Inspect their contents, if you wish, and lock them. Then pass them to us, and we will relay them into the boat. And then we will all get on board and be off. For Beirut."

I could not avoid the feeling that he had never told a lie before meeting me. I went to the trunk and Odon opened it with his key. I locked each box in turn and handed the boxes one by one to Odon's men, who carried them to the ship and came back for more. By the time I was handing over the final box, all of the men had managed to work their way onto the boat. Only Odon was left, and just as I passed him the final box, a man called his name from the ship.

"Ah," he said, "there seems to be trouble on board. Wait right here, I'll be back in a moment."

"I'll go with you."

"Oh, it's not necessary. Ah, what's that down there?"

I looked where he pointed. He had picked up the tire wrench and he telegraphed the blow so completely that it took a certain amount of effort to let him hit me at all. But he got me—going away, just a glancing blow on the side of the head. It hurt and it staggered me, and I followed through and sprawled in the sand.

It occurred to me as I lay there that there was a glaring flaw in my plan. Suppose he hit me a second time while I lay there like a lump? Suppose he very neatly caved in the back of my skull?

A glaring error. But, after all, I was new at this sort of thing. In any case, Odon didn't try for a second shot. Perhaps he was as unused to hitting people as he was to lying. He dropped the tire iron, tucked the strongbox under his arm, and ran to the ship.

I did not move an inch until the ship was out of sight.

175

17

I got into the car, a Chevrolet about ten years old, and I understood it well enough. They had been kind enough to leave the keys in the ignition. I turned the car around and drove back to Balikesir, found the house, pulled into the garage, and closed the door. I had work to do. Fortunately I had plenty of time to do it.

Because they would not open those strongboxes until they reached their destination, which would take a day at the least. They wouldn't open the boxes because they would not trust one another well enough. As long as the locks were unimpaired no one would be able to remove some of the gold before they got back to Sofia and split it into their unrightful shares.

I could see them all, gathered in Father Gregor's comfortable house, ceremoniously unlocking or breaking open the padlocks, lifting the lids of each box in turn, and finding nuts and bolts and files and weights and nails and screws and rusty hardware of all sorts. Some six hundred pounds of rusty hardware, by my own admittedly rough estimate. Six hundred pounds of scrap metal, some of it lying loose, some of it neatly wrapped in ancient cloth bags and leather pouches. But all of it junk, and all of it theirs, and not a scrap of gold anywhere.

I had presented my unofficial resignation from the Society of the Left Hand. It bothered me in a way—it was, as well as I could remember, the only organization from which I had ever resigned.

But it did not bother me very much.

The gold was where I had left it, piled under a tarpaulin in the farthest corner of the garage. I used a variety of tools to open up the door panels of the Chevy and packed the door solid with gold coins. I stowed more of them under the seats, inside the cushions, under the trunk lining, and on top of the hood liner. It took several hours to pack the car properly. I did not want anything to rattle too obviously. A certain amount of rattling was perhaps inevitable, but one expected rattles in a ten-year-old automobile. I used newspaper and rags to muffle the more obvious rattles, tightened the car up again, patted the fender gently, and went back into the house.

I found a razor and some soap. I got out of my clothes, bathed, shaved, and put my filthy clothes on again. I would have preferred clothes that looked as though they might normally be worn by someone prosperous enough to own a car. I thought of buying some clothes before I left. There would be time for that later, I decided, when I was well out of Balikesir. In some other city, where police were not schooled to be on the lookout for Evan Tanner, I could more safely prepare for the rigor of a border examination.

I went back to the car. The Turkish passport and the Turkish driver's license were in the glove compartment. Odon had no further need of them, just as he had no further need of the car or of me, and so he had abandoned

177

us all together. I drove out of Balikesir. I drove south and east and south and east and I kept driving for a very long period of time. The roads were bad, and the car would not go over forty miles an hour without the front end shimmying madly. I stopped every fifty miles for oil. From time to time I grabbed a sandwich or a cup of coffee, then got behind the wheel and went on driving endlessly south and endlessly east.

According to the speedometer, I logged about eight hundred miles all told. I drove nonstop for almost two full days. In Antakya, in the southeast corner of Turkey, I finally purchased some decent clothes. I paid for them with gold pieces, which occasioned a certain amount of interest, but gold is apt to circulate in that corner of the world, and the merchant was more interested in cheating me than in calling the gold to the attention of the authorities.

I had no trouble at the border. I did not particularly resemble my passport photograph, but no one particularly resembles his passport photograph, and I drove from Turkey to Syria with little difficulty. I headed due south through Syria, hugging the coast, and had even less trouble passing from Syria into Lebanon. The Customs guards checked my car well enough, but they had no particular reason to take the doors apart, so they didn't. They looked in the spare tire, they rummaged through the glove compartment, and they let me go.

They missed the gold, the secret documents, and the fact that I was not the person whose passport I carried. Aside from that they didn't miss a trick.

I stayed at a good hotel in Beirut and put my car in the hotel garage. I told the bellhop that I was interested in finding a reliable gold merchant, and I tipped him a sovereign. Within an hour a young Chinese came to me. Did I have gold to sell? I said that I did. Would I accept

178

fifty dollars an ounce? I said that I would not.

"How much, sir?"

"Sixty."

"That is high."

"It is low. You would pay sixty-five if I insisted. Tell your boss that I do not bargain. Tell him sixty dollars an ounce."

"How much gold, sir?"

"Six hundred pounds."

"Six hundred pounds sterling?"

"Six hundred pounds of gold," I said.

He did not wink, he did not blink, he remained wholly inscrutable. He left, he returned. "Sixty dollars an ounce is acceptable," he said.

"May I meet your boss?"

"If you will come with me."

I went to a very modern office in a very modern downtown building. A Chinese in a London suit sat across the desk from me and worked out the details with me. I was a very difficult bargainer at first. After the fun and games in Turkey I had given up trusting anyone. But we worked out the arrangements. Several of the Swiss banks maintained major branches in Beirut. I need only open an account in one of them, a numbered account, and the Chinese would deposit funds in my account equal to sixty dollars an ounce for my total consignment of gold. His company had a warehouse where we would have sufficient privacy. I drove the car there, and several of his employees unloaded the gold from the car according to my directions. It was all weighed and tallied before my eyes. I have been unable to decide whether or not the scales were dishonest. On the one hand, the gold merchant seems to have been exceptionally honest, ethical, and scrupulous. But, at the same time, any man's honesty seems apt to bend when the stakes reach sufficient height.

It made no difference. He could cheat me an ounce on the pound, and it would still make no difference. Because the gold weighed out at five hundred seventy-three pounds and four ounces troy weight or 6,880 troy ounces.

"I will allow an average of .900 fine for the gold," he told me. "It is coin gold. Some is finer, some not so fine. Some no doubt is counterfeit. Neither of us has the time to check each piece, is it not so? It will be checked before it is sold, and my firm will either gain or lose depending upon the assay. If you insist, we will assay it before paying you, but it would force you to remain in Beirut for another week at the very least. For this reason—"

"Your terms are satisfactory," I said.

"You wish payment in Swiss francs?"

"Will the bank accept dollar deposits?"

"Of course."

"Is it convenient for you to pay in dollars?"

"Of course."

"I would prefer dollars."

"Of course."

The rest was mechanics. I fully expected someone to attempt to cheat me out of the whole bundle, but no one did. We went to the Beirut offices of the Bank Leu. I opened a numbered account and received a very involved explanation of the precise manner in which the numbered accounts operated. No one, I was assured, would ever know of the existence of the account or the balance in it without my express permission. No government on earth could obtain such information. I and only I could make withdrawals from the account. I would, however, be paid no interest. He wanted me to realize that I would be paid no interest.

That, I said, was quite all right with me.

We concluded the transaction. The Chinese merchant took all the gold away—he would eventually realize approximately fifty percent over and above expenses on his investment. I did not begrudge him the profit. The bank would also make out handsomely, carrying a huge account and paying no interest on it. I did not begrudge the bank their gain, either.

I had on deposit precisely $371,520.

I took a hundred dollars of this incredible sum in cash. I went back to my excellent hotel. In the clothing shop downstairs I bought a suit of clothes, a shirt, a suit of underwear, a pair of socks, and a pair of shoes. I added a tie, cuff links, and a belt. I went upstairs and bathed and dressed and had a huge and excellent dinner in the hotel restaurant.

There was only one thing left to do. After dinner, and after I had spent about an hour resting as completely as possible on my most comfortable bed, I left the hotel and took a taxi a few blocks farther down the street. I got out of the cab in front of the American Embassy. It was late in the afternoon, almost time for the Embassy to close for the day.

I walked up the steps. The late afternoon sun was hot. I opened the door and stepped into the utter luxury of genuine American air-conditioning. It made me more honestly homesick than I could have imagined possible.

A young man sat behind a large desk in the hallway. I stood in front of his desk for several minutes before he raised his neat head from the pile of papers in front of him.

He asked if he could help me.

"I hope so," I said. "You see, I've lost my passport."

"Oh, *have* you?" He rolled his eyes, signaling his

181

great irritation at stupid tourists who lost their passports.

"I suppose this happens rather often," I said.

"*Too* often. *Far* too often, to be frank. The absolute importance of keeping one's passport handy..."

I let him go on for quite a while. It was not an unpleasant lecture. I wish I could remember all of it.

Finally he found the appropriate form, poised a pen, and looked up at me.

"I don't suppose you remember the number?"

"I'm afraid not."

"No, naturally you don't. It never occurs to anyone to jot down their passport number. Not sufficiently important." He sniffed. "Your name?"

I paused, perhaps for dramatic effect.

"Oh, come now," he said. He was really incredibly snotty. "Now, don't tell me you've forgotten your name as well?"

"My name is Evan Michael Tanner," I said. "If you've forgotten it, I don't think you have much of a future with the State Department. I suggest you get off your ass and tell your boss the name of the stupid tourist who's been taking up your time. Evan Michael Tanner. You go tell him Evan Michael Tanner is here, and you see what he says."

But he remembered the name. It was delicious to watch his face mold itself into one expression after another. He reached for a buzzer and rang for the guards. We waited for them to come for me.

It didn't get at all rough until they got me back to Washington. The guards kept me under surveillance until the snotty kid could report to someone higher up, and eventually some men more important than he came to interrogate me. They assured themselves that I was really

182

Evan Tanner, found out that I was, and conducted me to a windowless room on the second floor. A guard made sure that I was not carrying a weapon. I was not. Then two of them stood in front of me while I sat in a swivel chair.

"There's a report that you had the British plans," one said.

"I do."

"You have them with you?"

"Yes."

"At this moment?"

"Yes."

"Care to turn them over?"

"If you'll show me CIA identification."

"I'm not CIA."

"Then get someone who is."

They got someone who was, and I solemnly took off my jacket, unbuttoned my shirt, loosened my undershirt, and came up with the packet of papers the tall man had passed on to me in Dublin. The CIA man checked them out.

One of the State Department men asked if everything was there.

"I don't know," the CIA man said. "I have to use a phone."

He went away. I sat with the two men. They offered me cigarettes, and I said I didn't smoke and finally I remembered to tuck in my shirt and button it up and put the jacket on again.

The CIA man came back and said that as far as he could tell everything was there.

"I don't know how the guard missed it. He frisked him for a gun."

"Well, it wasn't a gun," the CIA man said.

"Still, he should have found it."

"Forget it." The CIA man turned to me. "Of course, those could have been copied," he said.

"True."

"Were they?"

"No."

"Why the hell did you come here, Tanner? I don't get it. Who are you working for?"

I didn't say anything.

"What do you expect, a pat on the head and a ticket home? Did you know that you started six international incidents all by yourself?"

"I know."

"I was just on the phone to Washington. They want you sent there in a private plane under a quadruple guard. Today, they said. We can't get hold of a private plane today."

"When, then?"

"Christ, I don't know. Maybe tonight, maybe tomorrow morning. Who knows? Tanner, you honest to God amaze me, you really do. How in hell did you wind up in Beirut? I wish I knew more about you. I know you're hotter than a grenade with the pin out and I know part of where you've been, but I don't know the rest of it. Why don't you tell me about it?"

"No."

"They'll ask the same questions in Washington. Make it easy for me. Brighten my day."

"I can't."

"Did you really start a revolution?"

I didn't answer that or any of the other questions he asked me. The whole business was very frustrating for him. He knew that I would be sent to CIA headquarters in Washington and that he would never find out the answers to any of his questions. The agency might keep him busy, but evidently he didn't often run into anything

184

as exciting as me and he was all curiosity, and I wasn't helping him a bit.

They eventually locked me into the room with a double guard. The guards were decent enough fellows. The three of us played hearts. I won about seventy cents, but I refused to take the money. It didn't seem right, somehow. After a few hours the CIA man came back with a few other men, and they handcuffed me rather elaborately and drove me to the Beirut airport. There was a smallish jet waiting at the runway. They loaded me into it along with four guards and the CIA man, and we took off for Washington.

No one had brought anything to read. Anyway, with the handcuffs on I couldn't have turned the pages. It was a very boring trip.

18

The jail cell in the basement of CIA headquarters in Washington was far more comfortable than the dank dark room in Istanbul. It was well lighted and very clean. There was a bed, a small dresser, and a shelf of paperback books. The books were mostly spy novels, I discovered. This struck me as very funny at first, but after I'd read them one after the other as one day followed another I lost sight of the humor of it all. It began to get to me after a while. I read the same spy novel twice and didn't realize it until I was within twenty pages of the end.

The meals were good. Actually, there was no single dish that was as good as the pilaff I had had in Istanbul, but there was a great deal of variety in the cooking, and I'm sure the diet was more nutritious than toast and pilaff and pilaff. The only aspect of the two weeks I spent there that became absolutely unbearable was the endless routine of questioning. It went on and on, and they seemed determined to keep it up forever. It was the complete reverse of Istanbul—there I had been ignored, left entirely alone for days on end, and here I was questioned morning and noon and night, questioned endlessly, and over and over, until I was certain that the next session would be the one to break me.

"Who are you working for, Tanner?"

"I can't tell you."

"Why?"

"Those are my instructions."

"We're more important than your instructions, Tanner."

"No, you're not."

"We're the U.S. Government."

"I'm working for the Government."

"Oh, you are? That's very interesting, Tanner. You're working for the CIA?"

"No."

"For whom, then?"

"I can't tell you."

"The U.S. Government?"

"Yes."

"I think you're crazy, Tanner."

"That's your privilege."

"I think you're full of shit, Tanner."

"That's your privilege."

"You say you're working for the U.S. Government?"

"Yes."

"What department?"

"I can't tell you."

"Why? Because you don't know?"

"I can't tell you."

"Who's your boss?"

"I can't tell you that, either."

"Tell me something about this agency, Tanner. Is it like CIA?"

"In a way."

"You can't tell us the name?"

187

"No."

"Can you tell us somebody who works for it?"

"No."

"Suppose we give you a phone. You call somebody and make contact, okay? And then they can come and spring you, and we'll all be happy. How does that sound, Tanner?"

"No."

"No? Why the hell not?"

"I was instructed not to make contact."

"So what the hell are you going to do? Sit here forever?"

"Sooner or later I'll be contacted."

"How? By voices talking to you in the night?"

"No."

"Then, how, Tanner? Nobody knows you're here. Nobody's going to know unless you tell them. There were no leaks in Beirut. You came here on a hushed-up flight, and the CIA alone knows you're in Washington. Now, how in hell is anybody going to get in touch with you?"

"They will."

"How?"

"I can't tell you."

"I can't tell you, I can't tell you, I can't tell you. Like a broken record. Tanner, you son of a bitch, that's the whole trouble, you bastard, you can't tell us a thing. Who gave you those papers?"

"I can't—"

"Shut up. Why did you turn them over to us?"

"Those were my instructions."

"Really? I thought you couldn't give us a thing, Tanner."

"I was told to deliver the papers to the CIA if I could find no other alternative. It would have been better to

188

deliver them to my superiors, but I could find no way to get into the country except through the American Embassy, and that meant delivering the papers to you. I was supposed to do it only if there was no other choice open and I couldn't contact my own group or get to the States under my own power, so I gave the papers to you."

"Were they copied?"

"Not while I had them."

"Where did you take them?"

"I can't tell you."

"Were you on other business? Or were you just cruising around Europe with the papers in your pocket for a couple of weeks?"

"I can't tell you."

"You're a son of a bitch, Tanner. I don't believe a word you're saying. We'll keep you here until hell freezes, do you know that? Take him back to his cell. God, he gives me a pain—"

Well, what else could I do? I know they didn't believe me. If they had swallowed my story, I would have doubted their competence. It was, admittedly, an absurd story.

But what else could I do? I had to get back to the States. It was my home, for one thing, and for another I was finding it increasingly exhausting to be on the run. I could not endure being a hunted man forever. Obviously I had to go back home and had to straighten everything out, somehow.

And so the story. I was working for a governmental agency, it was secret, it was important, and the CIA didn't know about it. I couldn't make contact, I couldn't give out information, I couldn't do much of anything but sit on my cot and read spy novels or sit on my chair and say "I can't tell you" until everybody got sick of listening to it. I had no idea what would happen eventually. I did not particularly want to think about it. It seemed impossible that they would let me go, and it was even less likely that they would release me to another country, or bring me to trial, or—

I couldn't imagine what they would do to me. Unless they would merely keep me in my cell forever, and that did not seem very likely. Sooner or later they would tire of questioning me. And then what? Would they release me?

They might. Not in a matter of weeks, perhaps not in a matter of months, but sooner or later they would tire of housing me and realize that I was not going to tell them anything more than I had already told them. Their attempts to trap me in questioning sessions were getting nowhere. Whenever I was asked anything remotely tricky, I merely announced that I could not tell them the answer. It was an umbrella for every possible sort of storm. They couldn't trap me. They couldn't get anything out of me. They couldn't do a thing.

Once I made a mistake. I asked one of them when they would let me go.

He grinned. "Tanner," he said, "I can't tell you."

I laughed. Actually, I figured I had it coming.

"Tanner, would you like to know something? I'll tell you something—we almost believe you. Almost. Why don't you help us out?"

"How?"

"Give us one name. That's all, one name. Just one person we can call up and find out if you're really you. Just one little name, Tanner, and maybe you'll be able to get out of here."

"I can't."

"A phone number, then."

"No."

"Tanner, I realize that you're gung ho. I realize you're loaded up to your old wazoo with esprit de corps and all that. We're very tall on those commodities around here, as far as that goes. God bless the agency, and long may she wave. And you probably feel the same way about your own group, right?"

"So?"

"What I'm getting at, Tanner, is we're all of us willing to die for our country. And we're even willing to go through hell for CIA. But there are certain contingencies, Tanner, that are not covered in the rule book. You don't want to spend the rest of your life rotting in a stinking cell when your own people are a few blocks away and all you got to do is holler. You know something? They're probably desperate for you to get in touch. They're probably beginning to worry about you. Why not let me call them for you?"

"No."

"Give me the initials, Tanner. Just the initials."

"No."

"It's all a big lie, isn't it? You a communist, Tanner? Or just a nut?"

"No."

"I don't believe a word of it, Tanner. Not a word."

"That's your privilege."

"You'll stay here the rest of your life. The rest of your goddam life. Is that what you want?"

"No."

"Well, how the hell will you get out?"

"My superiors will have me released."

"How will they find you?"

"They'll find me."

And they did.

• • •

191

They found me after breakfast. I had been in the jail cell for over three weeks, and by then I was past the point of wondering how long I could hold up under questioning. I knew by then that I could hold up forever. The questioning had tapered off now. Sometimes two or three days would go by without a session, and the sessions themselves were getting shorter and less vicious.

Until one morning after breakfast a guard came and turned the key in my cell door. One of the CIA men was with him. "They've come for you, Tanner. Get your things."

What things? All I had were the clothes I was wearing.

"And follow me. They found out you were here, finally. God knows how. I guess we've got a leak we don't know about. You come with me. You know something, Tanner? I didn't believe they'd ever come for you. I didn't believe there was anybody to come. I thought you'd sit in that cell forever."

"So did I."

"You can't blame us, you know. Put yourself in our position, you'd have done the same thing. Am I right?"

"You're right."

"So you don't blame us?"

"Of course not."

"Some of the things we said—"

"Just part of the interrogation. Forget it."

"Well, okay, Tanner. You're all right, Tanner."

Two men in dark suits were waiting in the front lobby. One of them said, "Phil Martin," and extended a hand. I shook it. The other said, "Klausner, Joe Klausner," and I shook his hand.

"The Chief just heard about you," Martin said. "It took us a long time. You've been here three weeks?"

"About that."

"Christ."

"It wasn't so bad."

"I'll bet," Martin said. "The car's out front. The Chief wants to see you right away. There's a bottle in the car if you want a drink first. You look as though you could use it."

There was a half pint of blended whiskey in the glove compartment. I took a long drink, capped it, and put it back. The three of us sat in the front of the car with me in the middle. Phil was driving. Joe turned in his seat as soon as we had pulled away from the curb. He stared out the back window.

After a few blocks he said, "Yeah, they're following us. Two cars double-teaming our play. A brown Pontiac and a light gray Ford. See 'em?"

"Uh-huh."

"Goddam CIA. Tell you the truth, I'm happy to see 'em there. If they're tailing us, it means they still don't know where our offices are. Which is just as well. Lose 'em, Phil."

"There would have to be two of them. Those boys don't even go to the john by themselves."

"So just lose 'em."

Phil lost them. He went around blocks, dashed the wrong way on one-way streets, and shook both our tails in less than ten minutes. "It's a hell of a thing," he said, "when you have to worry more about your friends than your enemies. The Chief is very anxious to see you, Tanner. He didn't know you were one of ours. He suspected it when we got rumbles about the bit in Macedonia. Dallmann had contacts in Macedonia. Dallmann's dead, you know."

"I know."

"Well," Phil said.

We rode the rest of the way in silence. Phil dropped us in front of a shoe-repair shop in a Negro slum. Joe and I entered a building by the door to the right of the shop and climbed three flights of squeaking stairs to the apartment on the top floor. He knocked. A deep voice invited us inside. Joe opened the door, and we went in.

Joe said, "Here's Tanner, Chief."

"Good. Any trouble with CIA?"

"None there. They followed us, but Phil outran them. He's good at that."

"Yes," the Chief said. "He's a good man."

"You want me to stick around?"

"No, that's all, Joe."

"Check."

Joe left and closed the door. The Chief was a round-faced man, bald on top, with fleshy hands that remained in perfect repose on the desk in front of him. The desk was empty of papers. There was a box labeled IN and another labeled OUT. Both were empty. There was a globe on the desk and a map of the world on the wall behind him.

"Evan Michael Tanner," the Chief said. "It's a pleasure to meet you, Tanner."

We shook hands. He motioned me to a chair, and I sat down.

"Dallmann's dead," he said. "I suppose you knew?"

"Yes."

"Shot down in Dublin, ironically enough. It must have happened just after he passed the papers to you."

I nodded.

"I suspected you might be Dallmann's man when we first began to get reports on you. We're not like the boys at the Central Intelligence Agency, you know. I don't believe in teamwork. I never have. It may be useful in some types of operations, but not in our type. Do you follow me, Tanner?"

"Yes," I said.

"I encourage my men to develop their own operatives. Keep them secret, don't let me know about them. When one of our men goes out on something, he goes alone. If he's in trouble, he can't call for help. If he's caught, I don't know him. So I didn't know you were one of Dallmann's group. I suspected it, as I said, but I wasn't sure. I became somewhat more certain when we received reports of the incident in Macedonia." He smiled for the first time. "That was excellent work, Tanner. That was one of the neatest bits of work in years."

"Thank you, sir."

"It may well turn out to have been the biggest wedge driven in Yugoslav hegemony since the end of the war. They were astonished when that revolt broke out. Astonished. The last thing anyone expected was a blowup in Macedonia. I know Dallmann had things planned in that area. I suppose that was why you made your first trip to Istanbul?"

"That's right."

"And of course that fell in. Brilliant work of yours, picking up Dallmann in Dublin afterward. And then having the nerve to carry through with the Macedonian plans. Most men would have settled for the British papers and brought them straight home. Dallmann would be proud of you, Tanner."

I didn't say anything. Dallmann—the tall man—must have guessed I was on his team from the Istanbul fiasco.

The Chief looked down at his hands. "Strange situation in Ireland," he said. "The Irish filched that set of plans out of London as neat as anything. The British didn't even know who had them. But we knew and we couldn't let them stay in Irish hands. Irish security isn't the best in the world, you know. And those plans were fairly vital. Dallmann took them away in a matter of days. Another power could have done the same thing.

195

We had to do the job first for two reasons. To get them away from the Irish and to teach Downing Street an important lesson in security. First nonsexual security scandal they've had in some time. Ought to keep them on their toes, don't you think?"

We both got a good laugh out of that one.

"The CIA give you a hard time, Tanner?"

"It wasn't too bad."

"You don't sleep, do you? Got that from your records. That must come in handy."

"It does."

"Um-hum. Imagine it would. Sorry I had to put you through three weeks of CIA interrogation. Understand you didn't tell them a thing."

"I had to give them the plans."

"Well, that was all right. Couldn't be helped." He chuckled. "You must have given them the willies. You know their standard interrogation procedure? Nothing fancy, just let a man fall asleep, then wake him up and question him, then let him drift off to sleep again, then more questioning. They hit you at your weakest point that way. But they couldn't do that to you, could they?"

"No."

"Very handy. Never thought of insomnia as a survival mechanism. Very interesting."

"Yes, sir."

He got to his feet. "You have contacts with fringe groups and nut groups throughout the world, don't you? Professional? Or a sideline?"

"Just a hobby."

"Valuable one, isn't it? You do much work for Dallmann?"

"No. Just incidental work before this job. Nothing important."

196

"Suspected as much. And yet you maintained discipline all the way, didn't you? And handled yourself like a professional. Very interesting."

For a long moment neither of us said anything. Then he came around the desk, and I got to my feet, and we shook hands again.

"What are your plans now, Tanner?"

"I'll go back to New York."

"Back to business as usual, eh?"

"Yes."

"Good. Very good." He thought for a moment. "We might have a piece of work for you now and then."

"All right."

"We're hell to work for. I don't know exactly what sort of arrangement you had with Dallmann. Doesn't much matter now, does it? But we're very hard masters. We give you an assignment and that's all. We give you no contacts. We don't smooth the way for you a bit. But at the same time, we don't ask for reports in triplicate. We don't want to know what you did or how you did it. We just expect you to deliver the goods. If you get caught somewhere, we never heard of you and you never heard of us. We can't even fix a parking ticket for you. And if you get killed, we drink a toast to your memory and that's all. No group insurance. No full-dress funeral with burial in Arlington. Understand?"

"Yes, sir."

"So you might hear from us some time. If something comes up. Sound good to you?"

"Yes, sir."

"I like your style, Tanner. Especially in Macedonia. That was quite a performance." He smiled again briefly, then turned aside. "You'll find your own way out. Walk a few blocks before you catch a cab. Might as well go straight back to New York. Don't ever try to contact me. I suppose you know that much, but I'll say it anyway. All right?"

"All right."

"How are you fixed for money?"

"I could use plane fare. I'm out of ready cash."

"Besides that."

"I'm all right." I thought for a moment. "I managed to . . . uh . . . pick up a little for myself this trip."

He laughed aloud. "Just like Dallmann," he said. "He never even put in for expenses. Said he made a neater profit than we could ever pay him in salary. I like to encourage that sort of thing. Teaches a man to think on his feet. You'll fit in fine with us, Tanner."

He gave me two hundred dollars for the plane and incidental expenses. We shook hands a third and final time, and I let myself out.